Praise for Josh Lanyon's
Come Unto These Yellow Sands

"Josh Lanyon doesn't just top the A-List—he IS the A-List when it comes to blending wit, suspense and romance. Mr. Lanyon's at the top of his game in *Come Unto These Yellow Sands*, an unforgettable story that will keep you entranced from beginning to end..."

~ *Romance Junkies*

"It is difficult to write a character whose addiction is convincing and have the reader believe both in his redemption and an HEA for the romance, but you pull it off in this novel. Swift is a fascinating character; his weaknesses and his strengths seem so intertwined, as if they flow from the same personality traits."

~ *Dear Author*

"*Come Unto These Yellow Sands* is well written, has deep, intriguing characters, a well plotted mystery and is filled with deceit, betrayal and fear. What more could you ask for? Oh, yeah. A satisfying end... you'll get it."

~ *Literary Nymphs*

"Josh Lanyon truly is a gifted writer and *Come Unto These Yellow Sands* is captivating from beginning to end."

~ *SensualReads.com*

Look for these titles by *Josh Lanyon*

Now Available:

The Dickens with Love
The Dark Farewell
Strange Fortune

Crimes & Cocktails
Mexican Heat
(Writing with Laura Baumbach)

Holmes & Moriarity
Somebody Killed His Editor
All She Wrote

The XOXO Files
Mummy Dearest

Print Anthology
To All a (Very Sexy) Good Night

Come Unto These Yellow Sands

Josh Lanyon

SAMHAIN
PUBLISHING

Samhain Publishing, Ltd.
11821 Mason Montgomery Road, 4B
Cincinnati, OH 45249
www.samhainpublishing.com

Editing by Sasha Knight
Cover by Kanaxa

First Samhain Publishing, Ltd. electronic publication: June 2011
First Samhain Publishing, Ltd. print publication: June 2012

Dedication

To Emmy Frost, who—maybe by accident—helped me choose the next adventure.

Chapter One

It was like those old Choose Your Own Adventure novels.

You are primary unit commander of the Lazarian Galaxy Rapid Response Team—

Well, no. Not that adventure. This adventure started: You are a respectable college professor and the director of the prestigious Lighthouse MFA program of Casco Bay College in Southern Maine. You have had one hell of a day and you just want to go home and enjoy a glass of wine and a nice meal with your lover—sort-of lover—Police Chief Max Prescott. But as you approach your office in Chamberlain Hall, you spot a kid slumped in a chair outside the door. Even from this distance you can see that the kid is having a worse day than you. If you want to do the responsible, grown-up thing, keep walking. If you want to make life easy on yourself, turn around and leave before he notices you.

Once upon a time, it would have been no choice at all. But Swift was older now—against the odds—and he took a certain pride in the fact that he no longer ducked out on his responsibilities. Besides, he recognized that tall, dark and despondent figure. Tad Corelli was one of the most gifted students to take part in the Lighthouse residency program. He reminded Swift a little of himself at that age—minus the self-importance and mile-wide self-destructive streak.

Swift found his keys as he reached the door. He glanced at Tad. "Sorry. I was held up. Have you been waiting long?"

Tad lifted his head, and Swift dropped his keys. "What the hell happened to you?"

Tad wore a dark coat and a black knit cap. The cap framed a bruised and battered face. One eye was swollen shut, his bottom lip was split and puffy, there was a crust of blood beneath one nostril. He bent painfully and retrieved Swift's keys.

Swift took them automatically, still staring.

"I'm okay," Tad mumbled. He looked at the door, clearly waiting for Swift to open it, and Swift shoved the keys in the lock and pushed the door open.

His office was a comfortable clutter of books and plants and old posters. The desk was an antique. It had belonged to Carl Sandburg. The leather chair behind the desk had belonged to Swift's own father, the poet and dramatist Norris Swift. The chair in front of the desk was a comfortable secondhand club chair. Swift put a hand on Tad's shoulder and guided him to its beige plush depths.

Tad leaned forward, head in hands, and Swift closed the office door.

"Do you need—what do you need?" He was at a loss. Physical violence was not his area of expertise, though he'd had the shit kicked out of him on occasion. But then he'd generally had it coming.

"Nothing." Tad looked up, met Swift's eyes and managed a gruesome smile. "You should see the other guy, Professor Swift."

"What happened?"

Tad put cautious fingers to his split lip. "Doesn't matter.

Look, I-I have to go away for a while. Please don't drop me from class. Or the Lighthouse program."

"Where are you going?"

Tad shook his head.

Swift sat on the edge of his desk, trying to read Tad's face. "It can't have been much of a fight. Your knuckles aren't banged up."

"Please..."

"What?"

Tad said pleadingly, "I just have to get away for a little while. I'm not dropping out. I just need time to get myself together. Just a couple of weeks or so."

Swift said slowly, "Okay."

At Tad's look of surprise, Swift said, "I'm not going to drop you, Tad. I want you in the program. But why don't you tell me what's going on? I might be able to help."

"No one can help." Tad closed his eyes, struggled with his emotions.

So much pain there. But then being young was a painful state.

"Is there anything you need? Do you have money? A place to stay?"

Tad's head moved in negation.

Swift gave it some thought. *Pay it forward.* He was alive today because people who didn't have to had taken a chance, had reached out to help him when he needed it most—not just once, but several times in his misspent youth. He leaned over his desk, pulled out the top drawer and fished around for the spare key to his bungalow.

He withdrew his wallet, rifled through it. He never carried a lot of cash. Not anymore. It was too dangerous. He'd got out of the habit—one of a number of habits he'd got out of. "I can give you twenty bucks and you can stay at my place on Orson Island while you figure out what you're doing."

Tad opened his eyes, his expression one of disbelief. "I don't...know what to say."

"You don't have to say anything. I've been where you are. Just take the time you need, get your head straight and come back ready to get to work."

Tad stared at him, unmoving, doubting.

"Okay?" Swift asked gently.

Tad nodded. He reached for the keys and the cash, shoving them automatically into his coat pocket. He put both hands on the edge of Swift's desk and pushed to his feet.

"You sure you don't need a doctor?" Or maybe an ambulance. The kid was moving like he was a hundred years old.

Tad shook his head.

"Let me know how you're doing, okay?"

Tad jerked another nod. He shuffled toward the door. Hand on the knob, he stopped. "Thanks, Professor Swift," he said without turning around.

The next moment he was gone, the door closing softly behind him.

Swift lived in an old deconsecrated church in the village of Stone Coast. Against expectation, it was a comfortable and practical living space, yet it still retained its original eccentric charm.

The original arched entrance doors, complete with stained-glass panels, were still intact. Gothic windows offered warm eastern light in the morning. The thick exposed wooden beams, floors, ceilings and even walls were all of dark, burnished wood. In place of the altar was a long marble-topped island within the raised, completely modern kitchen. Swift was a devout cook. For him, cooking went beyond therapy.

Speaking of religious experiences, the pews were also long gone—all but one which was positioned in the entryway. Swift had purchased a number of statues and carvings, large and small, from garden centers, estate sales and church auctions, and these now decorated the main living area. The stone fireplace and built-in bookcases were part of the renovation, as were the slate floors in the kitchen and entry hall. The upstairs loft with its giant master bedroom and bath was surrounded by ornate reclaimed 1940s' cast-iron railing. Upstairs the stained-glass windows were nearly intact. A giant cast bronze statue of a winged woman gazed down at the living room with a benevolent smile.

Swift was not particularly religious, but he experienced good vibrations in this old house of worship. It was a peaceful place, and he had needed peace when he'd arrived in Stone Coast fresh out of rehab six years earlier.

Arriving home after the meeting with Tad, he poured himself a glass of wine, one—he was careful about that—and started dinner. He wasn't sure if Max was dropping by that night or not. Max came and went as he pleased, which was how they both liked it, although Swift wouldn't have minded more coming than going.

He blended lemon thyme and pistachio nuts in the food processor for the pesto, drizzled in the olive oil and added freshly ground black pepper. As he worked, he thought about Tad. A smart, talented kid, but he hadn't been in any fight. He'd been beaten. Badly beaten. And he'd been scared.

But you couldn't force help on someone who didn't want it. No one knew that better than Swift. So you did what you could do. And maybe time and space was all Tad needed. Swift took a sip of wine, set the pesto aside and prepared the chicken.

Chicken with lemon thyme pesto and summer tomato salad. There would be plenty of food if Max dropped in. And if not, there would be plenty of leftovers.

Swift was reading *Passionate Hearts: The Poetry of Sexual Love* when he heard Max's key in the front door just after nine that evening. His heart sped up as it always did, and he spared himself a wry smile. What was it T.S. Eliot had written about when the here and now cease to matter?

At one time he'd tried to convince himself that his feelings for Max were more about being one of the only two openly gay guys in a small town, but in the last year or so he'd come to accept that he cared for Max. More than Max cared for him. For Max it probably *was* mostly about the fact that they were the only two openly gay guys in a small town. And whatever Swift had once been, he was entirely respectable now. He was a good catch. Except, as Max occasionally pointed out, he wasn't trying to catch anything. Max wasn't into commitment.

"Something smells good," Max said from the entryway.

Swift tossed the book aside and sat up. "Hungry?"

"Starving." Max appeared in the arched doorway, and Swift rose to meet him. Max was six four and broad-shouldered. His wavy hair was brown with reddish glints, his eyes were hazel. He looked a lot like Tom Selleck except for the devilish white scar through his left eyebrow courtesy of a coked-up would-be carjacker who had tried to carve Max's eye out.

Swift wrapped his arms around Max's neck. Max pulled him closer, and as Swift's mouth found his, he muttered, "But it'll wait."

His face was cold and he tasted like too many cups of coffee, but Swift didn't mind. He loved the taste of Max. He kissed him more deeply, melting inside as Max responded hungrily. It probably had to do with the poetry book he'd been reading before Max showed up. He'd definitely been in the mood and getting ready to deal with it himself. But here was Max with his big, hard hands digging into Swift's ass as he pulled him closer still, and Max's tongue licking at Swift's lips. Swift opened to that tentative probe, and Max's hot slick tongue slipped inside.

Swift moaned low in his throat. He wanted this—he always wanted this—and the best part was Max seemed to always want this too.

They continued to kiss, then Max broke for air. "I don't know if it's you or the fact that I haven't eaten since breakfast, but I'm getting lightheaded."

Swift laughed too, let his fingers tangle briefly with Max's as he led the way past a seven-foot-tall marble angel, its sword upraised, up the two steps to the kitchen. "You came to the right house, Chief. What d'you want to drink?"

"What's on tap?"

"Casco Bay Riptide Red and Summer Ale."

"I'll have a Red."

Max leaned against the doorframe and sipped his beer while Swift pulled the leftovers out of the fridge and heated the chicken.

"Tough day at the office?" Swift asked when the silence had stretched. Max appeared to be a million miles away.

He looked up, smiled faintly. "Yeah. You could say that. We don't get a lot of homicides. Maine's got the third lowest violent crime rate in the nation, and we've got one of the lowest rates in Maine. We're proud of that."

"You have a homicide case?"

Max nodded. "A local restaurant owner by the name of Mario Corelli was found shot to death on the beach at Wolfe Neck."

Swift's finger froze on the microwave start button. "What?"

"If you owned a TV, you'd have heard all about it. Mario Corelli. Corelli's Ristorante. We've eaten there a couple of times."

"I remember. The manicotti was incredible. Ricotta, mozzarella, pine nuts, herbs and a marinara sauce I'd kill to have the recipe for." Swift was answering automatically, giving himself time to think.

"Maybe that was the motive. Should I ask if you have an alibi?"

"You don't have a suspect?"

"We've got a couple of suspects. Corelli fired one of his waiters last night and the guy is missing. Also missing is Corelli's son Tad."

"Is Tad a suspect?"

"The kid and Corelli fought like cats and dogs. We definitely want to have a talk with him. The fact that he's disappeared is suspicious."

"Maybe he doesn't know about his father."

"Maybe." Max sounded skeptical.

"He could be missing for other reasons, right?"

"Sure." Max leveled a direct look from beneath his brows. "But his disappearance is news to everyone who knows him. The kid's been in trouble before. Substance-abuse problems, that kind of thing."

It was the wrong thing to say. Swift could feel his resistance building. "People can change."

"So the bleeding hearts tell us." As though he realized how harsh that sounded, Max added, "You're one of the rare ones, Swift."

Swift pressed the button and watched the microwave vibrate. He stared at his reflection in the microwave door. His face was a pale blank. There was just the shine of his eyes, the gleam of his earring, the dark frame of his long hair.

"It sounds like you already have your mind made up."

"I have a hunch," Max said, and the assurance, the certainty, in his voice raised Swift's hackles. It wasn't logical, it probably wasn't reasonable, but that judgmental streak was one of the things that bothered him about Max. It was one of the ways in which they didn't mesh. Not at all.

He folded his lips against the unwise words. Watched the chicken spinning slowly on its plate in the microwave.

Max said, "Come to think of it, Corelli's in your residency writing program, isn't he? What can you tell me about him?"

If he was going to speak up, now was the moment. Max might be a little jaded, a little cynical, but he was a good cop. An experienced cop. And he thought Tad was guilty.

And Swift disagreed. Swift had hunches about people too, and they were usually right on the money. He knew Tad Corelli. Max didn't. Tad Corelli hadn't acted like someone who'd just killed his father. He had seemed afraid, but he had not acted guilty or like someone on the run. He'd been battered, bloody, emotionally exhausted...but none of that indicated he'd committed murder.

And Swift felt a bond with Tad. He had from the beginning, from the day Tad had begged to be enrolled in the Lighthouse program. The kid wasn't working on his master's, he hadn't

15

even graduated yet, but he'd pleaded to take part in the ten-day residency that took place each semester, and though space was as limited as the program was competitive, Swift had responded to that passion. He'd pulled strings.

Tad deserved a break. He deserved a chance to tell his side of the story, and it would look better if he came in on his own. That much Swift knew just from listening to Max talk shop on long winter evenings.

"Something wrong?"

Swift turned to face him. He was thinking quickly. He could go out to the island tomorrow and talk to Tad, explain to him what was going on—Tad probably didn't know his father was dead yet, and that terrible news would come better from a friend. Swift remembered only too clearly the pain of his own father's death. And the relapse into cocaine use that had followed.

He said slowly, "He's...gifted."

"They all are in that program, right?"

Swift nodded. "More gifted than usual. He's the youngest student we've ever had enrolled in Lighthouse. Although, technically, he's not in the program yet."

"That's right. I remember now. You let him take part in the conferences even though he's an undergraduate."

"Right."

"How's he doing?"

"He's excelling. He's an exceptional kid. Just the fact that he wanted into the program so badly before he was even eligible is...inspiring to me. As his instructor."

Max's expression was polite. He wasn't much for touchy-feely. "What about friends?"

"He hangs out with a couple of jocks. Hodge Williams and

Denny Jensen."

That raised some interest. "The Jensen that quarterbacks for the Brown Bears?"

"Does he?" Swift shrugged, and Max's mouth quirked in response.

"Unless there are two Denny Jensens at CBC, yeah. The kid's attracted some big league interest according to the local papers. He's captain of the sailing team too."

Swift didn't follow the local paper any more than he followed college sports. "I think they all played football in high school together."

"What about a girlfriend?" Max asked.

"Nah. I'm satisfied with you for now."

Max looked up in surprise.

Swift raised an eyebrow. "Are you interrogating me, Chief?"

The microwave pinged.

Max offered his slow, devilish grin. "Saved by the bell, Teach."

Chapter Two

You stare and stare in disbelief at the mirror. How could this have happened? YOU ARE A MONSTER!

Okay. Maybe not that bad, but you *are* lying to your sort-of boyfriend, and you might even be an accessory to murder after the fact, or whatever they call it. Max will undoubtedly know what they call it when he charges you for—

"If the teaching thing doesn't pay off, you could always get work as a chef." Max spoke through a mouthful of chicken and salad, interrupting Swift's thoughts. "This is great."

Swift smiled automatically. They sat at the table in the kitchen. The overhead light picked out the golden bubbles rising lazily in Max's glass, blanched the dark wood of the cabinets to the color of old ivory and threw the rest of the room into gilded shadow. The topic of Mario Corelli's murder had been temporarily shelved. Swift had seen to that, and he was doing his best to keep it off the table. He didn't want to lie to Max. One of the things he liked best about their relationship was that they didn't lie to each other.

Except...even if his decision to keep silent was more omission than lie, Max would view it as a lie of omission. Frankly, so did Swift.

"How was *your* day?" Max asked suddenly.

Swift shrugged. Max delivered an interrogative look, the

pale scar on his forehead crinkling.

Swift drawled, "Oh, you know. The usual whirlwind gaiety. Faculty meetings. Lectures on subjects only I find interesting. Being stood up for office appointments. Grading papers over a soggy avocado sandwich." He picked a cherry tomato out of the salad bowl and absently considered the sharp burst of pulpy flavor on his tongue. There was a time when something as mundane as the bite of tomato juice would have had him reaching for a pen, testing the first words of a new poem. Now flavor was an end in itself.

The aroma of the roast. Savor the moment.

"Avocado in November? You're an optimist."

"Probably."

Max's gaze was unexpectedly keen. "Getting bored with the academic life?"

"Nope." Swift meant that. He liked teaching. He liked believing that he was introducing some of these kids to neoteric ideas, fresh ways of looking at literature and even the world around them. And he took pride in his role as the director of the Lighthouse program. He liked the image of himself as a mentor rather than menace, and he believed that he had earned the title, that he had helped some of these aspiring writers reach—if not their full potential—greater potential.

He even liked the routine. Needed the routine, in fact. But...

"But?" Max was reading his thoughts tonight.

Sometimes it was a little dull. A little lonely. "Just looking forward to spring, I guess."

"You've got a wait. It's only turned autumn."

"True."

"Maybe we—" Max broke off. For a split second he looked

19

uncomfortable. Or as close to uncomfortable as Max got.

"Maybe we...?"

"Ought to finish up in here and leave the dishes for tomorrow."

"Sure." Swift didn't push. He never pushed Max. Instead he gave a slow, lazy smile and watched the color warm Max's face.

At the far end of the loft was a large painted mural of an undersea temple. Smiling dolphins swam through bands of sunlight and broken marble columns. Sand dollars littered the glittering ocean bottom with scattered gold coins and pearls. A solemn-faced Poseidon contemplated Swift over the glint of his trident. That would be Poseidon's trident, though Swift's was making an impressive showing too thanks to Max's generous attentions.

Max crawled over, stretching out beside Swift. Swift smiled up at him. He felt relaxed and at ease in the way unique to good sex with the right person. He felt content. What a lovely word that was. *Content.*

"God. You're..." There was a quiet sincerity to Max's voice.

When he didn't complete the thought, Swift raised his right eyebrow—something he'd spent an inordinate amount of time practicing when he was a goofball kid.

Max traced the haughty arch with his thumb. "Beautiful," he admitted self-consciously.

Swift spluttered into a laugh. "You need to get your eyes checked, officer."

"Hey."

"Hey, yourself." Swift wrinkled his face in distaste. "I look like an ex-ju—"

"You're beautiful." Max cupped the side of Swift's face, his own expression serious.

Swift crossed his eyes, trying to break the mood.

Max's lips twitched. He shook his head reprovingly and bent to press his mouth to Swift's. He was smiling. The smile imprinted itself gently on Swift's mouth. On his memory.

"What?" Swift asked when he could breathe again.

"You look like that angel in the front room."

Swift laughed, dismissing it. Secretly, he was flattered. He liked the jaded, world-weary expression of the angel in the downstairs alcove. He thought the statue had more than beauty. It had character—something he hoped he had developed by now.

Max rested his forehead against Swift's. They breathed in soft unison. At last Max groaned and lifted his head. "I've got to get some sleep or tomorrow's going to be hell."

Swift nodded. Tomorrow was going to be hell anyway, for a number of reasons. He was holding tight to these peaceful moments.

Max rose from the bed and padded off to the bathroom. Swift listened to him splashing and brushing and flushing. Max padded back to the bed, turned out the lamp and climbed in beside Swift who had already cocooned himself in the blankets. It was cold in the loft. The building's heating in general left something—about six degrees—to be desired.

Max tossed and turned a couple of times, and then, as he always did, settled on his side facing Swift. The shine of his eyes vanished. His sigh was warm against Swift's face.

Swift listened to Max's breath smoothing out, deepening. Moonlight lit the mural at the far end of the room, gleamed in the kindly eyes of the swimming dolphins, glanced off the spirals and curls of the ruined temples.

For a time Swift lay quietly, thinking. "Max," he said abruptly, "is it possible Corelli's death was an accident?"

"Hmm?"

"Could the gun have gone off by accident or something?"

Max mumbled, "What gun?"

"The gun that killed Corelli."

He could feel Max blinking, trying to gather his sleep-scattered wits. "He was shot three times in the chest. I don't think it was an accident."

"Oh. No. Doesn't sound like it."

"Why?" Max sounded more alert.

"Just thinking about Tad." That at least was the truth.

The bedclothes whispered as Max turned onto his back. "No point worrying about what you can't control."

"When did that ever stop anyone?"

Max chuckled sleepily and patted Swift's thigh beneath the bedclothes. "Night, Teach."

"Night, Chief." But it was a long time before Swift closed his eyes.

He woke to the familiar pleasure of muscular arms wrapping themselves around him, a hard body molded to his back, a very hard cock nudging his ass. But the mouth brushing the nape of his neck was very soft indeed.

Swift raised his lashes to read the alarm clock. Not quite forty minutes before they needed to leave this sweet, humid womb. He didn't move, didn't even let his breathing change. He savored the moment. Soon the day would officially begin and their brief allotment of intimacy would be a memory.

"Time?" Max's calloused hand raised goose bumps on Swift's sensitized skin. Max's hand slid lower, lower over the ridges of abdomen, the flat plane of Swift's belly.

"Time." Swift caught his breath as Max's fingers tangled in the softness of Swift's pubic hair. Max's fingers flicked him teasingly, and Swift sucked in his gut.

"Ticklish?"

Swift shook his head although they both knew he was extremely ticklish. His cock pushed for attention, and Max obliged, wrapping his fist around the thickening length.

"Good..." Swift breathed out as Max used his free hand to lazily tweak his nipple, "...morning."

"Could be at that."

Max's tongue rasped the back of Swift's neck, tasting his skin. Swift shivered, a full-body shiver that made Max chuckle, warm breath gusting against Swift's nape.

"Mm. I like that."

"You do. You're...what do they call it? Orally fixated. Licking, sucking, biting..." Max nipped Swift's shoulder, and Swift made a sound between protest and encouragement.

"Kissing..." gasped Swift.

"Kissing," agreed Max. He pulled Swift over, and their mouths latched on a wet, warm kiss, suddenly starving for each other. Ravenous. As though they hadn't just had each other a few hours before.

They broke apart, and Max gave Swift's cock another hard caress, skin on naked skin. "You know what I want?"

Swift closed his eyes, smiling, murmuring, "Mm. Me too."

Neither of them being kids or inexperienced, they had it down to a science. A fun science, though, like...zoology or astronomy. Max rolled away, dragged open the drawer in the

23

bedside table and grabbed the lube. Sea kelp and guava bark. It had provided Max no little amusement. It was nice stuff though, slick and slippery on Max's calloused fingers. It felt nice melting into Swift's body, it smelt nice mingling with the sharp scent of male sex.

Just the lube, no condoms. That was the closest they got to commitment. The acknowledgment that they were only sleeping with each other.

Max covered Swift's body with his own. Swift wound his arms around Max's broad shoulders. They gazed at each other in the dove-soft shadows of the loft. Their faces drew slowly close, their mouths met in a gentle graze, but the gentleness fell away in seconds to the brisk, efficient pursuit of satisfaction, kisses turning rough with bristly cheeks and hot tongues moving in the silent language. They explored the taste of each other as though somehow something might have changed overnight.

Max's hands locked on Swift's shoulders, and he sheathed himself neatly in Swift's body. Swift moaned. His hands gripped Max's muscular butt, pulling him close so that their hips ground against each other. They humped, frantic and without grace in the naked honesty of need. Then Max groaned into Swift's mouth, raw, male longing, and within seconds of each other they were spilling out their slickness, coating groins and bellies with hot wetness.

They rested for a few seconds, caught their breaths, and then they were up and moving through the morning routine of showers and shaves. Max kept a couple of shirts and changes of underwear at Swift's. He dressed while Swift made coffee and toast. No time for anything more. Not on the weekdays. Not even Fridays. On the weekends—well, they didn't spend that many weekends together. Swift wasn't sure why, exactly, but this one would be no different. He considered it while he buttered slices of oat nut bread, sprinkling his with cinnamon and sugar. Considered what he knew of Max.

Even after three years of seeing each other regularly—or at least what passed for regularly with the two of them—there was a lot about Max that remained a mystery to Swift. Initially, if Swift was honest, he hadn't been that interested. He'd just been grateful to find someone to have sex with who he could stand to talk to afterwards. After a year or so he'd grown more interested in who Max was when he wasn't with Swift, but he'd run into the amiable but impenetrable barriers Max kept firmly in place between them.

He knew the basics, of course. He knew Max was forty-five, in excellent health, had never been married, and voted Independent. He was easy to talk to and a good listener. He sang in the shower in a pleasant baritone and rarely got the words right. He couldn't cook to save his life but he enjoyed eating, and to compensate for it put in time at the gym and went running on the mornings he didn't wake up in Swift's bed. He followed sports—baseball and football in particular. He liked soul music. Most important, he had never heard of SSS and the last time he'd read a poem was probably in *Mother Goose.*

"I'll have to get mine to go," Max said, jogging down the staircase.

"Ready and waiting." Swift took a mouthful of coffee, watching—appreciating—as Max strode into the kitchen area. An ex-jock, Max moved well, with a careless, athletic ease.

Picking up his yellow mug, Max downed his coffee in three giant swallows. He scooped up the paper towel wrapping his toast, pausing in front of Swift long enough to give him a coffee-tasting peck.

"No cinnamon on mine?"

"Nope. Have a good day," Swift said.

25

"I'll see you."

Swift nodded. Max usually left it like that. Sometimes they made plans but just as often it was left to chance. The fact that chance usually led them to each other's bed might mean something—or it might not.

Today Max would be busy with his murder case.

And so would Swift.

Chapter Three

You are an underwater explorer. You've just accepted your most challenging assignment. To find the ancient vanished city of Atlantis lost far beneath the waves.

Or maybe you're just a sleep-deprived, under-caffeinated college professor with rain trickling down the back of your neck as you swim—er, sprint—from your car to your classroom clear on the other side of campus.

Normally Swift didn't mind the rain. He liked water. He'd been born underwater. His parents—literary icons Norris Swift and Marion Gilbert Swift—had wanted their only offspring to experience a childhood rich in sensory and cultural stimulation. They had documented, both in film and poetry, nearly every moment of Swift's childhood journey. From tadpole to poet in his own right, it was all there for anyone who wanted to know— and was a regular subscriber to PBS.

It was a peculiar thing to grow up in the public eye. It was a still-weirder thing to serve as the living, breathing form of inspiration for two of the greatest poets in North America. Sometimes, when Swift had been much younger, it had been hard to separate who he was from who everyone else thought he was. He'd seen home movies of himself at eighteen months sitting inside a giant watermelon and trying to eat his way out, of being dipped in watercolor and crawling over canvasses. He'd swum with dolphins at age eight and drank wine at his parents' dinner parties at ten. His godfather had been the Poet Laureate William Stafford, and according to family legend, Anne Sexton had once babysat him while Marion Swift was accepting a gold medal from the American Academy of Arts and Letters.

No wonder Swift had been doing drugs by the time he was seventeen.

That was the year he'd also scored the Agnes Lynch Starrett Poetry Prize for *Black Solstice,* his first book of poems. *BS*, as he'd come to think of it, had gone on to win the Kate Tufts Discovery Award. He'd followed that success a year later with *Cuckoo Shells*, which had pretty much summed up his state of mind. *CS* had been critically lauded but had failed to score any major awards. Swift had been certain his career was over. Maybe it would have been better for everyone if it had been.

He'd sought comfort in more chemical relief. A lot of chemical relief. By the time he was nineteen he had learned to deal with the crushing expectations of his nearest and dearest by means of his serious and less and less easily concealed cocaine habit.

But that was all a long time ago. Now days Swift was healthy, whole and mostly happy. And even if he never wrote another poem as long as he lived, he would be okay.

The only reason he was even thinking about this, dredging up painful history as he jogged across the green and glistening campus, was Tad. Swift didn't need to hear the particulars of the case—although it had been all over the local radio during his morning drive—to know it was possible Tad *had* killed his old man. Especially if the kid was using again. Personal experience. Swift always figured it was a miracle he hadn't killed someone—let alone himself—back in the bad old days.

Not that Tad had appeared high when Swift spoke to him the previous afternoon. In fact, Swift had never once picked up a hint that Tad suffered chemical addiction. But if Mario Corelli had delivered the beating Tad received? Yeah, Swift could see Tad hitting back.

Tad was a big kid. Not just tall but broad, heavyset. He reminded Swift of an overgrown puppy who still hadn't grown into his size. He'd played football in high school despite his current literary aspirations. Swift could imagine him striking out in anger and doing serious damage. Except Mario Corelli hadn't died in a fight. He'd been shot to death. Shot to death on a state park beach according to Max, which sort of eliminated the striking-out-in-blind-rage defense.

Swift wished now he had shut up and let Max talk about the case. No one else really had much information beyond the most basic, but rumors were already circulating that Tad was wanted by the police for questioning.

He reached Chamberlain Hall, which was busy and bustling at a quarter to eight in the morning, and picked up his messages and mail from Dottie Dodge, the department secretary. Dottie was a fierce munchkin of a woman, and she had never made a secret of the fact that she thought Swift did not belong at a fine old institution like Casco Bay College. The first week Swift had started teaching at CBC she had informed him that her nephew had died in a car accident caused by a drunk driver. It was Dottie's opinion that all addicts were the same animal and that that animal ought to be put down. He tried not to take it personally, although after six years of that same unbending attitude it wasn't easy.

That morning Dottie greeted him more cordially than usual, her yellow-green eyes alight with malicious pleasure as she handed over the usual assortment of junk-mail catalogs and brochures. Dottie religiously kept Swift's junk mail safe for him.

The important stuff she tended to misplace for a day or two.

Swift shuffled quickly through the envelopes. There was yet another letter from Shannon Cokely. Probably once again listing her imaginary grievances against the Lighthouse Program in general and Swift in particular.

"The police were here when we unlocked the doors this morning."

"Oh?"

"They made copies of Corelli's cumulative records." Dottie sniffed. "Looks like teacher's pet is in hot water again."

There was no point pretending he didn't know what she was talking about. The whole campus was abuzz. "I thought the cops were looking at a waiter Corelli fired."

"Oh, you're way behind the times. The waiter, Tony Lascola, has an alibi. And the Corelli boy has disappeared." She smiled tightly. Dottie had always been deeply offended by the fact that Swift had bent the rules to get Tad into the Lighthouse program.

"Innocent until proven guilty," Swift reminded her, he hoped affably.

Dottie gave another of those sniffs that conveyed so much disapproval with so little oxygen.

Nodding farewell, Swift headed for his office. He was running late and had just enough time to dump his coat and grab his roll book before getting over to the seminar room where his students milled restlessly in the hallway.

"Hey, Professor!"

"Morning, Professor Swift."

"Professor Swift? About Tuesday's assignment..."

He unlocked the door and let them crowd inside the room, absently responding to greetings and questions.

The first class of the day was Foundations of Literary Analysis. It was a class Swift enjoyed not least because it spared him teaching Introduction to Creative Writing. As sponsor of the college literary magazine he had all the exposure to newly hatched scribes he could handle. The course emphasized a subject dear to his heart: critical reading and writing. It never failed to dismay him how many kids confused liking something with literary merit. If there was one thing he intended his students to take away at the end of the semester, it was an ability to separate personal likes and dislikes from objective analysis.

It would probably be easier to teach them to write book reports in iambic pentameter, but he was going to do it or die trying. If there was one life skill everyone on the planet needed, it was the ability to think with critical objectivity.

As always, once Swift began his lecture, the passion for words and writing swept him away, and he forgot all about Tad and the murder of Mario Corelli, and the fact that Max was going to be very unhappy with him.

"The discovery that you like William Carlos Williams? That's great. We'll keep it in mind for Christmas. But to get an A on a paper in this class, you're going to have to convince me that you've got a good reason for liking William Carlos Williams."

He could see the faces of those most fond of their own opinions wrinkling up in protest.

"I want to see those opinions supported by evidence. I want you to prove to me that you've considered elements like theme, setting, characterization—"

"How can there be characterization in a poem?" objected Denny Jensen.

Jensen was a smart kid even if he had taken Foundations

of Literary Analysis in the hope of avoiding having to write anything himself. Swift remembered what Max had said about Jensen the evening before. He wouldn't have guessed Jensen was the bright hope of the football team given the fact that he exhibited none of that attitude of entitlement of so many jocks, so he forgave him the dumb question and was off and running, explaining *exactly* how characterization worked in poetry.

The next seventy minutes passed quickly—for Swift anyway. Back in his cubbyhole of an office he graded papers, absently listening to the drum of rain against the windows, and calculated how soon he could get out to Orson Island to talk to Tad. Not before his afternoon seminar. Not without bringing attention to himself.

That worried him—the realization that he was automatically thinking like a criminal. He wasn't a criminal. It wasn't even for sure that he was helping a criminal. He just wanted to make sure Tad wasn't sandbagged. What was wrong with that?

A little before lunchtime Dottie buzzed him.

"Bernard Frost," she announced.

It took Swift a few strange seconds to place the name. Recognition brought a little jolt with it. Bernie was Swift's agent. Former agent.

"You're kidding." That was a rhetorical comment. Of course Dottie wasn't kidding. Dottie had no sense of humor. She didn't bother to reply, and a split second later the phone rang in Swift's office.

Swift picked up. "Bernard."

No one called Bernard "Bernie". No one ever had but Swift who, back when he was a punk kid, thought it funny to irritate Bernard at every opportunity. What did it say about him that he'd set out to antagonize his own agent? His agent and his friend. He remembered once, after he'd been beaten up by a less-than-amused drug dealer, calling Bernard in the middle of the night—and Bernard had unhesitatingly answered that cry for help, driving to the rescue, cashmere coat thrown over his silk pajamas, hair sticking up on end like a cockatoo. Bernard had sat with Swift in the emergency room while they stitched the cut in his scalp and taped his broken nose.

So there was a lot of warmth in Swift's voice. There was warmth in Bernard's tone too, though he sounded tentative even after six years, always prepared to find that Swift had once more descended into self-destruction. "My dear. How are you?"

"Good. Very good. How are you?"

It was odd to be making polite chitchat with someone who knew him as well as Bernard did. Had. Sometimes you had to go through the ping-pong preliminaries. It had been nearly two years since they'd last spoken. They still exchanged cards at Christmas.

"I'm in fine fettle, Swift. As a matter of fact, I'm just back from a fabulous holiday in Barbados." Bernard forever sounded like someone who'd escaped from a Noel Coward play, like one of those suave congenital bachelors—and he *was* a congenital bachelor, but he was also as straight as a baseball bat.

"That must have been nice."

"Oh it was, my dear." Bernard launched into a wry and witty account of his island vacation. He followed that with a catty description of a literary luncheon he'd recently attended— Capote couldn't have done it better—complete with updates and the latest gossip about people Swift no longer gave a damn about.

Swift appreciated that this was all warm-up for the main event and waited patiently, if a little nervously. Bernard would not call just to chat. Not these days.

"But how did we get sidetracked on me when I rang to hear about you? I don't suppose you're...working?" The last word was cautious. Bernard didn't mean *working* as in teaching or being otherwise gainfully employed. He meant writing. He meant poetry.

"No."

"Not a word?"

"Not a word worth showing anyone."

"I only ask because Fountainhead has been in touch about the *Blue Knife* collection."

Swift sank back in the leather chair that had once belonged to his father. He felt...gut-punched. Fountainhead Press was a small, independent literary press. Best known for the prestigious Fountainhead Prize, it was one of the most influential publishers in the United States. Fountainhead had published all but Swift's first collection of poems.

After ten years Swift had nearly forgotten the plans for his last ill-fated collection. He'd sort of assumed Fountainhead had forgotten too.

When he found his voice, he said, "There was no *Blue Knife* collection, Bernard. You know that. We all know that. I lied to get an advance because I needed money for coke."

Bernard cleared his throat. "Er...yes." The discomfort traveled all the way from Midtown Manhattan. Such dangerous streets.

"Do they want me to repay the advance?" Swift couldn't even remember how much it had been. Nothing wildly extravagant, safe to say. Fountainhead was a small operation, and financing poets was never a huge moneymaker. Whatever the amount, he'd blown it—literally—within a week.

Well, his teaching salary wasn't exorbitant, but if

Fountainhead would give him a little time, he should be able to figure out a way to come up with the cash. If worse came to worse, he could approach his trustees—but that would be a last resort.

"No, no," Bernard interrupted his roiling thoughts. "Nothing like that. They just—well, we all—hope that you might be writing again."

"No." Swift made an effort to temper it. "Sorry. The words just aren't there."

Bernard didn't seem to hear him. "In fact, given the complicated circumstances, Fountainhead is even willing to kick in another grand."

Far from cheering Swift up, that news just made him feel all the more wretched. "That's generous of them, but I'm not writing."

"Ah." Bernard's careful tone was a dead giveaway. "What about the poems you wrote after...?"

Swift's heart paused mid-beat. He managed to say, "After what?"

"After Norris passed away."

Passed away. What a feeble term for a star collapsing on itself. All that light and brightness and warmth extinguished.

He closed his eyes, and over the sick, hollow pounding of his heart said hoarsely, "No."

"I'm sorry. What was that?"

"No."

"Why not let me look at them?" Bernard persisted. "They might be better than you think. They almost certainly are. You were always far too harsh a—"

The laugh that tore its way out of Swift's chest shocked them both.

35

But...truly? The poems he wrote after he learned his father had died? The poems that narrated the end of his two-year struggle to keep clean? The poems he wrote in that final, despairing plummet to self-destruction? How could anyone even ask?

"I can't."

"But—"

Just for an instant the close rein Swift kept on himself slipped. "No one is ever going to see those poems. Not while I'm alive."

Bernard's silence was stricken. He said, "Swift, dear boy. I didn't mean—"

"I know."

"I thought perhaps time had—"

"I realize. But no."

"Of course. It's completely your decision." Pause. "But the poems *do* still exist?"

If Swift started laughing, it was liable to turn into something else. He flattened all emotion out of his response. "Yes. And after I'm dead you can do whatever you like with them. You're my literary executor, Bernard."

"Don't joke about that."

"It's okay. I'm not planning on going anywhere. You're going to have a long wait to get your clutches on my greatest works."

He was trying to lighten the mood, but Bernard wasn't laughing. Maybe the bad old days when Swift's imminent self-annihilation loomed over their heads were still too close.

Bernard cleared his throat and said in apparent non sequitur, "I saw Marion in Bermuda."

"Did you?" Swift asked without interest.

"She was vacationing there with Ralph. She looks well."

Ralph. Swift stared out the rain-blurred window. "She always does."

Bernard's hesitation stretched the distance between them. "She seems happy."

"Good for her. Damn. There's the bell. I'll talk to you later, Bernard."

"Yes, all right," Bernard said hastily, "but Swift at least, well...at least *consider* Fountainhead's offer."

"I'll think about it," Swift lied.

There was no phone at the bungalow on Orson Island, and for the first time Swift regretted that. He wished it was possible to cancel his afternoon seminar, but sticking to his routine had become second nature by now. He didn't like to diverge from his road into the yellow wood. It always felt slightly perilous. More perilous some days than others.

Lunch was spent at a local coffeehouse grading more papers. There was a lot more grading papers in teaching than he'd originally anticipated. He didn't mind. He actually found a lot of the stuff kids wrote amusing. Had he ever been that young? That naïve?

He listened with half an ear to the conversations around him—most of which sooner or later touched on the murder of Mario Corelli. Corelli's restaurant was a popular and successful one, and its owner was well known in Stone Coast. His wife Nerine was currently running for mayor, although there was speculation that she might drop out of the race now.

Swift ate his clam chowder bread bowl, mechanically marked papers, and absorbed the delightfully shocked conversations flowing around him. Popular opinion was that Tad had killed his old man. Max was right. The Corellis hadn't enjoyed quite the warm relationship Swift had with his father, but that didn't mean Tad had killed Mario. It didn't mean that hearing about Mario's death wouldn't be a terrible shock. It didn't mean he hadn't loved his father.

Swift needed to get to the island and talk to Tad. He wasn't going to make his mind up about anything until he'd heard Tad out.

So he spooned his soup, graded papers and refused to think of anything else.

After lunch Swift returned to campus in time for his Reading Poems seminar. The Reading Poems course was always a mix of pleasure and pain. Pleasure because he did still passionately love poetry and the course covered a range of poetic practices and a variety of media. Pain because most of these kids read anything but their own work *very* badly.

There are few things in this life more bamboo-under-fingernails than good poetry read aloud badly—unless it is bad poetry read aloud badly.

Swift suffered stoically through renditions of Browning's "My Last Duchess" and Lowell's "Patterns", and the minute the classroom was empty, locked the door and bolted for the parking lot.

It was still raining as Swift's Jeep pulled slowly off the Casco Bay Lines ferry onto the sandy beach at Orson Island and headed up the winding road that led to the bungalow.

He'd inherited the bungalow from his father. Norris had lived there for several years before he met Marion Gilbert. It was on Orson Island that he'd written two of his most famous plays, *Name Dropping* and *Broken Bells*.

Technically, Orson Island was part of the city of Portland, Maine. It had a year-round population of 60. During the summer months the population swelled to 150. Swift's original plan had been to live on the island year round as part of his staying-clean strategy, but the ferry commute had proved too difficult, and though he liked his privacy and the idea that his father had intended that refuge for him, the island was too isolated.

Now days he used it for a vacation home or when he needed time on his own.

There were no paved roads on the island, but the dirt roads were hard-packed and wide. Swift drove them easily, despite the rain sheeting down. White sand, white skies...the only color came from the trees lining the road, scarlet and gold foliage fading into the autumn mist.

Nothing gold can stay...

How very true.

In the early 20th century the island and its quaint, cozy inns had drawn summer folk, but these days there were no hotels. Orson Island was not on anyone's Top Ten Vacation Getaways. A number of homes were seasonal rentals. Few people lived on the island year round. The only real public services were a post office located in Sandy's General Store and Café, a strictly volunteer fire department and a one-room local school. As far as luxury amenities, the island boasted a community hall, a lending library and a tennis court.

Swift turned off the main road onto a loose gravel drive which led to the bungalow. He could see the rooftop and chimney through the flame-colored trees. By now Tad would know he was coming. He'd be able to hear the car engine from a mile away. The island was very quiet, as Swift knew from his own experience, and this time of year the only sounds to break the silence were the rush of waves, the wind through the trees, the cries of gulls.

At last the bungalow swung into view. It was a 1920s bungalow, gray and white clapboard with a screened porch overlooking the bay.

Swift parked in the circle of shell and pebbles, and went up the stairs. The scent of autumn and burning leaves sharpened the damp air.

He knocked. There was no response from inside the bungalow. He gave it a few seconds and then knocked again.

When there was still no reply, he unlocked the front door and stepped inside.

He knew at once that Tad was not there. The tobacco-brown curtains were drawn across the windows, the fireplace was cleaned of all ash and laid in readiness, the dust on the tabletops was undisturbed.

"Tad?" Swift called against the sinking sensation in his gut.

The bungalow smelt cold and clammy and empty as seaside places did after being uninhabited for a month or two. Wherever Tad had gone after leaving Swift's office the previous afternoon, he had not come here.

Swift walked through the rooms, footsteps sounding troublingly loud in the extended silence. The paneled interior had been photographed many times, and as usual he had that odd sensation of seeing the past and the present overlap like double exposure on film. His father's battered typewriter—which had belonged to his father before him—sat on a small table facing the window overlooking the beach.

Outside the window he could hear rain ticking against a metal watering can.

Swift walked out to the back porch and gazed down at the

empty beach below. Cyan-blue waves ruffled against the sand and rocks. There was no sign of anyone.

A gust of wet wind blew against his face. Mother Nature giving him the raspberry. He shivered. Shining drops beaded along the edge of the porch roof and splashed down on the steps in moody silence. Swift turned and went back inside to have another look around, not wanting to accept the obvious: that Tad had never arrived. That Tad was missing—possibly on the run.

Possibly something worse.

There was a ring of undisturbed mold around the waterline of the toilet bowl. The fridge was empty of everything but a box of baking soda and an unopened jar of blueberry preserves.

The bedroom, too, had not been used since the last time Swift had stayed on the island. The wooden blinds were closed. The pale green chenille bedspread was slightly crooked. The white dresser top was cleared of anything but the milk glass shaded lamp and a framed photo of Norris Swift's parents, dead long before Swift was born.

The bed was one of those white antique storage beds with drawers built into the base and a bookshelf for a headboard. The shelves were crowded with Swift's childhood collection of Choose Your Own Adventure books. One of the books was lying on the bed. *Who Killed Harlowe Thrombey?*

Swift picked it up, opening to his forgotten bookmark, his smile dimming at the sight of a faded antique postcard featuring 19th century couples, parasols and Sunday best, strolling along the water's edge. Beneath the flouncing hemlines were printed the words: *"Oh! Come Unto Those Yellow Sands." Shakespeare.*

Max had sent him that card last summer when Swift had been staying on the island for a couple of weeks. He turned the card over. Max had written in his neat, controlled handwriting, *Wish you were here.*

That had to be the single most romantic gesture Max had made in the course of their relationship. It had been enough to get Swift to end his island retreat a week and a half early and head back to the mainland.

Max had been satisfyingly appreciative, but it had not been the turning point that Swift had privately hoped for. Max had been glad to see him—as he had been glad to see Max—and life had gone on as usual.

Standing in that silent, shadowy room, it suddenly hit Swift that it was probably too late now for things to move in the direction he'd have liked. Time and tide. Love had its own circadian rhythms, and it was beginning to look like he and Max had missed their chance, that they'd slipped into a comfortable somnolence. Perhaps they would continue on indefinitely, but it was all too likely one of these days they were simply going to drift gently, quietly apart.

That still might be preferable to the shrieking wake-up call Swift would have to deliver when he got back to town and told Max that he'd invited a murder suspect to stay at his bungalow—and that the murder suspect was now twenty-four hours further ahead in his escape from justice.

Chapter Four

You have wasted too much time. You must get back on track.
Should you phone Inspector Pennyfeather and find out whether
he has made progress on the case or should you proceed on your
own?

If you phone Inspector Pennyfeather, turn to page 47.

If not, turn to page 8.

Or maybe you should just take a minute or two to think it
out—seeing how much you've screwed things up already, you
fucking idiot.

Swift gripped the ferry railing and stared bleakly down at
the churning water. The rain had thinned out to a mist. It felt
good against his flushed face. He'd been too restless to stay in
his car, and he'd spent most of the trip back to the mainland
walking up and down the slick deck.

Despite the weather he was warm enough. He was wearing
the coat Max had bought him last Christmas. A hooded, lined
Carhartt. It was a nice coat though Swift didn't particularly care
about its breathability and waterproofing and all the other
things Max had mentioned when Swift opened the neatly
wrapped parcel. Swift was sensitive to the cold, and Max had
dealt with it in his usual efficient manner. Was that romantic?

Swift had given Max a seascape by Maine artist Caren-
Marie Michel.

Max had smiled over the gift, held it up and given Swift a quizzical look. He'd hung it in his bedroom.

Swift had wondered what they'd do for the holiday this year. He'd toyed with the idea of suggesting they go away for a couple of days, even if it was just spending some time alone on Orson Island, but he'd never quite had the nerve and now...now it might be beside the point.

Max didn't get angry easily or quickly, but when he was mad, he stayed mad. He would be angry about this, Swift had no doubt. He probably had a right to be angry.

The ferry docked on time at the terminal in Portland, and Swift headed straight back to Stone Coast.

If it were done when 'tis done, then 'twere well it were done quickly. There was Shakespeare for you. Not *The Tempest*. Not the stuff of golden sands and sweet sprites and wild waves. No. *MacBeth*. A nice, juicy crime story. A tale of murder and madness.

Perfect for the day Swift was having.

He cranked up the Muse CD in his player and pressed the accelerator.

Stone Coast was a scenic little village near Casco Bay not far from Wolfe Neck State Park. The town had retained its rustic charm and, barring the luxury cars in the driveway and a few coats of fresh paint, many of the houses looked as they had in the 1800s. The architects of the newer structures tended to follow the organic inspiration of Frank Lloyd Wright and Bruce Goff. There was a lot of money in Stone Coast. A lot of people were interested in seeing Stone Coast become to the arts what Freeport was to retail.

Swift drove down the shady wide streets, past the little shops and art galleries and comfortable homes to the small brick police station surrounded by tidy green lawns and a forest of wet flagpoles.

Inside the station it was warm and surprisingly quiet. Hannah Maltz, the dispatcher, was working at her computer, clicking briskly away at the keyboard. She was a very pretty middle-aged woman—far too pretty to be an effective cop, in Max's opinion. Max had a tendency to make those kinds of judgment calls. What Hannah thought about being regulated to desk duty was anyone's guess, but she was a great dispatcher. She had a very nice voice in an emergency. Not that Swift had many emergencies these days.

"Why hello, Professor Swift," Hannah greeted him. "Wet enough for you?"

Swift was unsure what official explanation of their friendship—if any—Max offered inquiring minds. Having grown up in the spotlight, Swift was basically blind to public curiosity. He took it for granted that people paid attention to what he did, and he'd stopped noticing his own celebrity a long time ago. After three much publicized stints in rehab you tended to develop a thick skin. But Max was the police chief of a small town, and it went without saying—or at least they had never got around to discussing it—that he required discretion.

He was not much good at jokey back-and-forth stuff, but Swift said gravely, "Are you checking out my gills again?"

Hannah laughed. "Chief Prescott's on the phone, but you can go on through."

The door to Max's office stood open. Swift could see a sliver of Max tilted back in his chair, phone to his ear. He heard snatches of Max's deep tones between the click-clacks of Hannah's keyboard.

Max glanced up as Swift pushed open the door. His brows rose in surprised inquiry, and he nodded to the chair in front of his desk.

"You can bitch about First Amendment rights all you want, Harry, but I'm telling you if you print that, we're going to have words."

Swift sat in one of the chairs before Max's orderly desk and looked idly about the small office with its battered file cabinets, wooden coat rack, bulletin boards and bookcase with leather-bound volumes that were older than Max.

Whatever Harry said on the other end of the line amused Max. He gave that deep, growly laugh that always sent a pleasurable shiver down Swift's spine. He wished Max would hurry up and get off the line. He hoped the phone call never ended.

The first time Swift had been to this office was six years ago, not long after he'd moved to Stone Coast. He'd woken one morning to find someone had plowed into his parked car during the night. He reported the hit and run and spent a couple of minutes talking to the then newly elected Chief of Police. The only thing he really recalled of that first meeting was that he'd immediately liked Max's air of quiet, easy competency. It hadn't occurred to him that Max was gay. Sex, let alone romance, had been the last thing on his mind in those early brittle days of his recovery.

"I'm just an overworked, underpaid public servant of the people." Max's eyes met Swift's and he winked.

That was another thing Swift remembered from that very first meeting. Max's unexpected charm. You didn't look for charm from a cop. Swift didn't, anyway. But Max had it in spades. It didn't hide the tough competency, just made it a little more palatable, like the spoonful of sugar that helped the medicine go down. As now. Harry—most likely Harry Wilson, editor of the *Stone Coast Signal*—was having the law laid down in the nicest possible way. And as pissed off as he undoubtedly was, he'd probably vote Max into office for a second term when Max came up for reelection in two years.

Hannah came in and left a sheaf of papers in the tray on Max's desk. "I'm taking off," she whispered to Max.

He raised a hand in absent acknowledgment. "Yeah, yeah," he said good-humoredly into the mouthpiece. "Same to you, my friend." He stood his pen on its nose, absently balancing it for a second, then catching it before it fell. "Sure, give me a call. Maybe sometime next week."

Swift smoothed his suddenly damp hands on his jean-clad thighs. The moment of truth. He wasn't ready for it.

After all, no one need know what he'd done. Even when Tad was caught, he might not say Swift had given him keys to the cabin. It might never come out at all.

But no. No. Swift no longer permitted himself to run from the difficult things.

Max hung up and smiled across his desk at Swift. His eyes were the warm color of good whisky. "Your timing is perfect. I've just got time to grab some supper before I have to meet the coroner." He rose, six foot four of lean muscle, and reached for his leather jacket hanging from the coat rack.

Swift stayed seated. "Max, I have to talk to you."

"Something we can't talk over while we eat?"

"Indigestion guaranteed."

Max took a closer look, scrutinizing Swift's face. He slowly sat down again. "Okay. Shoot."

His heart was hammering with something weirdly close to panic. Swift made himself go on, made himself speak calmly. "I neglected to tell you last night that I'd seen Tad Corelli earlier. In the afternoon. After my classes were finished. In fact, I loaned him the keys to my place on Orson Island."

Max didn't move a muscle. He didn't even blink. He was so still, Swift wondered if he'd heard.

He opened his mouth to ask, but Max finally said in a voice stripped of any emotion, "You didn't think that was something you ought to mention?"

"Yes. But...I wanted to talk to him first. I wanted to convince him to give himself up." Swift watched Max reach for the phone. "He's not there now."

"And you know that how?"

"I went out there this afternoon. There's no sign that Tad ever arrived at the bungalow."

"You... Jesus fucking Christ." Max let the handset drop back in its cradle. He stared at Swift. "Are you *crazy*?"

Swift shook his head, though the question was probably rhetorical.

"You knowingly, *deliberately* let a murder suspect..." Max's voice died out as though his thought process had short-circuited. He continued to gaze at Swift in almost stricken disbelief.

"I didn't know he was a suspect when I offered him the use of the bungalow."

"You sure as hell knew after I told you last night."

"I'm sorry," Swift said. "I acted on instinct. Maybe a bad one."

"Maybe? *Maybe?* Do you have any clue of what you've done?"

Unwisely, Swift protested, "Even if Tad did this, it's not like he's Public Enemy No. 1. He's a confused, scared—"

"Don't." It was enough to shut Swift up. Max's face was white, his eyes blazing with fury. He looked like a stranger. A

48

stranger Swift would not want to get on the wrong side of.

"Max—"

"Not one fucking word more, Swift."

But there was always room for one word more, right? Especially this word. Besides, Swift had always been so very bad at following rules.

"I'm sorry, Max," he repeated.

Max stared at him as though Swift had been hand delivered by Martians. As though Swift were an alien creature that Max needed to exterminate—as soon as he figured out whether to use bullets or pesticide.

"Yeah?" Max made a funny sound that wasn't quite a laugh. "Not as sorry as you're going to be."

The hair rose on the back of his neck. Swift searched the hard, implacable planes of Max's features. Max wasn't a guy for idle threats. "Are you...? Am I...?" He wasn't even sure what question to ask. He knew that expression although Max had never worn it before—not for Swift. It was the expression that said, *You're pathetic. You're a junky low-life loser. You can't be trusted. You aren't one of us. You don't belong here.*

It was an expression he'd have done anything to keep from seeing on Max's face.

Almost anything.

Swift steadied his voice and got out, "Am I...under arrest?" He tried to say it without emotion, but he had at long last reached a point in his life where he had something to lose. A number of things, in fact, that he didn't want to lose. Wasn't sure he could survive losing. Arrest meant losing them all.

Max didn't seem to hear the question. He was on his feet again, moving into action, speaking under his breath as he grabbed the phone. Tight, fierce words. "Stupid, arrogant, irresponsible, crackbrained…" He jabbed a couple of buttons and then paused. Fastening that lightless gaze on Swift's face, he said, "Get the fuck out of my office. Get out before I do something we'll both regret."

Swift was up and to the door when Max threw after him, "You realize this is probably going to cost you your job?"

Swift had no answer. Or maybe the answer was in his face. Max turned his back on him and snapped his orders into the phone.

If he had it all to do again…?

Well, that was the point of those Choose Your Own Adventure books, right? Taking responsibility for your decisions, living with consequences. The lady or the tiger? You never knew until the door swung open.

If Swift could hit instant replay of the previous evening, he'd do it differently. He'd probably speak up when Max mentioned Mario Corelli's murder. Speak up and ask that he be allowed to go to the island first to speak with Tad, to break the news about Mario—and, if it wasn't news, to convince Tad to give himself up.

But unfortunately you didn't get multiple do-overs in real life, and it looked like Swift had seriously, fatally screwed up. But one thing you learned in rehab, there was no point bewailing the pratfalls. The only thing that mattered was getting back up again.

The faster the better.

Was there a way to fix this? Beyond apologizing again to Max when he had cooled down, Swift couldn't think of one. If he knew where Tad was, he could do what he'd planned on this afternoon, but he had no idea where the boy might hole up—and any ideas he came up with were bound to be things the police had already thought of.

Swift left the police station, drove home on automatic pilot and headed straight for the kitchen. After some aimless opening and closing of cupboards, he decided to prepare a bacon quiche. Not because he was hungry—the smell of the browning bacon had him gagging over the trash bin—but because the dish was complicated and required his full attention. He needed distraction from his worries and he needed routine, so he rolled out the pâte brisée, eased the dough into a 9-inch fluted tart pan, whisked the eggs with the cream, milk, salt, pepper and nutmeg. And when it was all done, when the quiche came out of the oven golden brown and flaky and smelling of warmth and earth and light, he made himself sit and eat.

Beyond the importance of routine, it was vital to stay healthy in times of stress. Swift had badly abused his body for most of his life. His current state of health required consciousness and commitment. He allowed himself two glasses of wine with his meal. The second glass of wine was a compromise. For the first time in a long time he wanted something else—wanted it badly.

That was a natural reaction to emotional strain. The best thing was to ignore it and stay busy, so after dinner he built a fire in the fireplace, put on a Barber CD and settled on the sofa with the latest stack of submissions to the *Pentagoet Review,* the college's quarterly poetry magazine.

Since Swift had taken over sponsorship, the magazine had doubled both in size and circulation. Granted, that wasn't saying a whole hell of a lot. It was still a mostly obscure college publication. The people who had hoped they might discover a new poem or two from SSS had long given up, but the magazine continued to thrive and Swift was proud of it.

He flipped through the first couple of submissions—calligraphy on colored paper, no less.

He was never very popular around submission time, but whether anyone noticed or not, he'd considerably eased his critical standards over the years—*had* to in order to fill the pages with something other than artwork. Even so there were limits.

That aching hollowness is filled when you are near. When you are far away my soul pores forth...

Soul pores. He sighed and turned to the next submission. The trouble was most of these kids—and more than a few of his colleagues—were used to the generally uncritical praise from a circle of writing friends.

Blame is the flame of a candle made of stone. I love you thrown in vein...

He glanced at the byline. Tess Allison had been the magazine's faculty advisor before Swift had come along, so that "vein" was probably deliberate. Either way this one would have to be published. Swift had learned a few things through the years—generally the hard way.

He turned to the next submission—all lowercase. This one was a clever take-off on E.E. Cummings's "since feeling is first..." which happened to be a favorite of Swift's.

since feeling is first

who pays any attention

to the syntax of things

will never wholly kiss you;

Wonderful. And this little parody was wonderful too. He read it over twice. Smiling, he set the submission in the pile with the others marked for acceptance. Nothing made him happier than when he found a jewel like this.

Mostly what he got was the inevitable adolescent and post-adolescent angst usually written in anticipation of coitus and punctuated with "I, I, me, me, I." Sunset, suicide and long walks on the beach figured largely in the variations on the theme of nobody loves me, nobody understands me, we're all gonna die.

No wonder his thoughts kept circling back to Max's office. Each time he remembered the angry contempt on Max's face, heard that whiplash *get the fuck out of my office,* it was all he could do to keep down the boiling acid of his dinner.

Crackbrain. That pretty much summed it up. How had he not realized ahead of time what a disastrous decision he was making by not telling Max what he'd done? Apparently it was only too true about the permanent brain damage cocaine caused.

He let his head fall back on the arm of the sofa and stared up into the soaring cathedral ceiling past the grid work of blackened beams into the ink shadows. He couldn't let himself think about Max. The rest of it was already more than he could deal with. If he was arrested...if he lost his job...?

Either one of those was liable to prove too much for his fragile equilibrium. He knew better than anyone how weak he was, how...untrustworthy. His relationship—friendship—with Max was one of the things that gave him the most happiness, most comfort. No, he couldn't even consider that loss right now. Not on top of the rest of it.

Swift jumped up, scattering the neat stacks of papers. He circled the large room, too nervous to stay still any longer. He needed...something.

Maybe a walk.

The rain had stopped. The cool air would feel good after an hour of sitting so close to the fire. He could stretch his legs, fill his lungs, clear his head.

He started toward the coat hook by the door but stopped.

No. No, leaving the house now was not a good idea.

Swift mentally ran through The List. The list of ways he'd found of coping when the craving started. The first version of the list had been supplied by his therapist. Since then he'd had six years to come up with his own personal tried-and-true methods of distracting himself from that twisting, gnawing hunger. In the beginning he'd resorted to elaborate diversions: hyperbaric oxygen treatments, infrared sauna, acupuncture and massage therapy. Now days a long walk was one of the best things, but at night...no. The night offered the wrong kind of possibilities. Sex was a good distraction and comfort, but the only person he wanted to have sex with was Max. And jacking off on his own was a poor substitute for that.

He could usually find some relief in small, homely things like a cup of hot tea and calming music, a hot bath and aromatherapy candles, looking through art books, meditation and visualization techniques. *Martha Stewart Living* magazines. He had a whole collection of them. There was something very comforting about Martha's ruthless discipline and focus— something almost Zen. And there was always yoga. Yoga and meditation.

He couldn't stand the thought.

It was disheartening to realize that he'd come to take his focused well-being so much for granted that he felt unprepared to deal with the sudden resuming of the symptoms of addiction.

Not that Swift had been silly enough to think he was cured, but after six years he'd reached a point where dealing with his habit was no longer the mainstay of his day. What had triggered the craving? The phone call from Bernard? The fight with Max? All of it? None of it?

Whatever the reason, he now needed a distraction. Nothing that was going to trigger anxieties or put him in temptation's path. He went into the kitchen and fixed a cup of chamomile tea, carried it back to the cluttered comfort of his office and sat down to sort through the papers and books and brochures he tended to stockpile.

He didn't let Mrs. Ord in this room to tidy up, or he'd never manage to find anything at all—not that he spent a lot of time in here. Mostly he worked in his office on campus or at one of the local coffeehouses. When Swift did work at home, he tended to sprawl on the sofa in front of the fire or, in better weather, on a lounge chair in the garden.

Looking around at the stacked books and piles of paper, he tried to decide what needed doing first. His gaze fell on the bookshelf and a familiar spine. He rose and pulled the narrow volume out. *Black Solstice* by SSS. Sebastian Shadrach Swift. His mouth quirked. Now there was a moniker. From the time he had been old enough to speak, he'd insisted on being called only Swift.

He flipped through the crisp pages curiously, studying his own adolescent efforts. It had been twenty years since he looked at these.

Time roaring loud behind me,
Spring-heeled sun sprinting over housetops and dusty trees;
And there they are, glistening, brilliant, motionless,
Dying stars stitched in a failing sky
By mild and faded fingers long since turned to dust.

He snorted. What the hell was that supposed to mean? He'd have been better off writing about walking with his boyfriend on the beach.

Swift stared moodily at the black bird-scratchings on the snowy page. An idea suddenly came to him. Tad had submitted a poem to the magazine, hadn't he?

Swift shuffled more stacks of papers, moved more books. Where the hell...?

He opened one of the deep desk drawers and swallowed at the unexpected sight of a blue rigid paper box laminated with images of clouds and crimson leaves. He'd forgotten that was in there.

He stared down at the box. What a weird coincidence that Bernard should be asking about those poems. To this day he didn't know who had collected and saved them after he'd ODed.

He closed the drawer with a little bang and kept moving papers and files until he found the folder with the twenty lonely accepted submissions to this spring's *Pentagoet Review*. He flipped through them until he found Tad's submission.

Cast your shadow white as stone

Wing of laughter, heart of bone...

Thirty lines of it beneath the title "Ariel".

Ariel.

Was that Ariel as in homage to Plath? Or Ariel the asexual sprite from Shakespeare's *The Tempest?* Or Ariel as in a real, live flesh-and-blood girl?

Because if this Ariel did exist, there was a slim chance she might know where Tad was. Assuming Max hadn't already tracked him down and was holding him in a jailhouse cell. In which case it was too late for Tad.

And perhaps too late for Swift.

Chapter Five

You're journeying on your own by train through the snowy mountains of Romania. This lonely and remote range is known as the Carpathians, and this part of the country is rumored to be the ancestral home of vampires!

Although, in fairness, most of the kids weren't that bad. You couldn't go by the fact that they all looked dazed or half-dead on a Monday morning. He probably didn't look a hell of a lot better after the weekend he'd had.

The good news was he hadn't been arrested. He had half expected it, but there had been no word from Max at all—that, of course, was also the bad news.

Not that Swift had sat around waiting to hear from Max. He'd managed to keep himself occupied planting over two hundred Asiatic lily bulbs in the back garden. He'd dug holes and raked leaves and mulched until his back felt ready to break. Then he'd cleaned out the garage, giving away boxes of books and odds and ends of old furniture and fixtures. He got rid of the bike he never used. He got rid of the punching bag that only Max used. He should have slept like a log, but the nights had been spent tossing and turning as he went over and over the scene with Max in his office.

But better not to think about Max just now.

Swift said briskly, "At the outset of *The Tempest* we see

Prospero as man in conflict. He's wise, balanced, mature, but he also longs for revenge—although I guess we can argue that it's justice he longs for. He's not a man of perfect judgment. He lost his position of political authority by failing in his duties. Now he's got one chance to revise that mistake. He doesn't create the opportunity, it comes 'by accident most strange' and 'a most auspicious star'. So sorcerer or not, Prospero's not all powerful and he's not in total control. He plans to reverse his fortunes and regain his previous position, but there's no guarantee of success. His plan might not work. It's dependent on timing. On Fate."

In the back row, Hodge Williams's head tipped back, and he woke himself up with a loud snort.

"Wouldn't you say so, Mr. Williams?" Swift inquired, just to be a prick.

"Uh..." Hodge sat up, blinking. There was a ripple of laughter around him.

After a second, Hodge laughed too. He was a nice kid. Not the brightest bulb, but handsome and—for a varsity-jacket jock—good-humored. He was also one of Tad's closest friends.

What Hodge and Tad found to talk about was a mystery, but plenty of friendships had been built on having only one thing in common. Swift could testify to that.

Tad would need a friend about now. According to the news on the radio that morning, he was still on the run four days after his father's death. Swift decided to have a word with Hodge after class. It couldn't hurt, right? He dearly wanted to find a way to fix things.

Claudia Lambert raised her hand. Swift nodded permission.

"I saw the film *The Tempest*. It was with Helen Mirren. They changed Prospero to Prospera." Claudia stuck her tongue out. She had an unusually long tongue. Swift observed it, fascinated.

"Uh...did they?"

"It was *terrible*."

Because Prospero was now Prospera? If that was the case, he could only imagine what snake-tongued Ms. Lambert would make of Derek Jarman's untraditional version.

Swift turned back to the chalkboard and out of the corner of his eye caught motion at the door.

Glancing over, he saw Max standing just inside the classroom.

His willful heart gave a delighted leap before he recalled the situation between them. Max's face was impassive, and Swift's throat tightened with a painful mix of fear and longing. Was this it? Was the arrest he had feared all weekend now imminent?

Several of the students were throwing Max curious glances. Max was impervious to them. He nodded curtly to Swift, apparently giving him permission to continue with his lecture, but no way could Swift calmly conduct class while wondering if he was about to be led off campus in handcuffs.

That morning he'd told himself on the drive to work that he was prepared for anything. He wasn't.

How could you prepare for something like this?

He shot a glance at the clock in the back of the room. "I think that's it for today. You should have read up through act four, scene one by Wednesday."

There were a few surprised faces, but mostly everyone was moving fast, gathering notebooks and backpacks before he could change his mind. Cell phones flipped open like transporter devices used by space crew desperate for escape. The seminar room doors flew open and students began to file out.

"Hi," Swift said to Max who had not moved.

"Swift." Arms folded, Max continued to wait, unsmiling, as students moved between them on their way to the door.

Yes, this was clearly going to be official business. Not that he'd really hoped for anything else. Except that you always hoped...right up to the moment the axe fell. Swift carefully stowed his lecture notes and roll book away in his briefcase and sat on the edge of the desk, waiting.

Max didn't move a muscle until the last student had shuffled out. Then he pulled the door shut.

"Tell me if you're going to arrest me," Swift said. "My nerves can't take this."

The look Max gave him was unmoved, but what he said was, "Arresting you isn't going to solve anything, and it would only bring more unwelcome attention from the media our way. That's the last thing we need now."

There was no hiding his relief, and Swift didn't bother to try. "Thank you."

"Don't thank me, because if it made sense, I'd throw your butt in a cell in a New York minute."

Swift nodded. It was too hard to meet Max's steely gaze. He stared at the well-worn carpet. Institutional blue. Why did everyone, from mental hospitals to jail visitation centers, favor that same depressing shade? Why not a soft, buttery yellow? Or the fragile pink of a baby's blanket? Granted, belfry blue ought to be his favorite color by now. He'd seen enough of it in his lifetime.

It occurred to him that Max was expecting more of a response. "Have you found Tad yet?"

"No. That's why I'm here. I need to ask you some questions about what happened between the two of you." Max added acridly, "I should have held you for questioning Friday, but I admit to being thrown off-guard."

Max's brown boots appeared in Swift's line of vision. He looked up. Max stopped a couple of feet away, propping his arm on the lectern. Max was keeping a safe distance. Possibly to control the desire to throttle Swift.

"Tad was in class on Thursday. He seemed...well, I didn't notice anything out of the ordinary. When I saw him later, he'd obviously been in a fight. Bloody nose, black eye, split lip. He said I should see the other guy."

Max's dark brows drew together. He considered. "What time was that?"

"After four. It might have been as late as four thirty. We had a department meeting, so I'm not sure how long Tad was waiting."

"What about the department secretary? Wouldn't he have checked in with her?"

"Anything's possible, but I doubt it. We try to encourage it, but students don't really need to make appointments. The idea is instructors keep regular office hours and make ourselves available to students. Tad might have asked Dottie where I was but, like I said, he'd been beaten up. I don't think he wanted to advertise that. Plus, I think it had just happened."

"Why's that?"

"He hadn't had time to clean himself up at all. Tears and blood." Swift's mouth crooked. "Been there, done that."

"That doesn't mean anything."

Swift shrugged.

"Tad said *you should see the other guy.* Did he give you any clue to who the other guy was?"

"No." Swift thought that over. "Did it look like Corelli had been in a fight?"

"No."

"But—" Swift tried to read Max's face. "Doesn't that prove that Tad wasn't fighting with his father?"

"It doesn't prove anything. It means Tad might have been lying about getting in a few good licks of his own."

Swift remembered his own observation that Tad's knuckles weren't bruised or cut. Either he hadn't fought back or he'd been jumped. "Okay, but what about Corelli's hands? Were they banged up? Because maybe Tad wasn't in a fight with him at all."

"The two things don't necessarily have anything to do with each other. If Corelli beat the kid, there might have been some defense argument in there, but the fact that Tad got in a brawl with someone else doesn't mean he didn't pop his old man. He threatened to kill him the night before, according to his stepmother."

"But you can't go by that. People say things in anger. Friday night you were probably mad enough to—" He broke off.

"I wouldn't go there if I were you," Max said.

Swift's face warmed. "Maybe the timing of this fight gives Tad an alibi. When was Corelli killed?"

"We're withholding that information for now."

Swift ignored the painful implication that he was no longer trustworthy. "So it's possible Tad has an alibi?"

"It's possible." Clearly Max thought the possibility slim. "Before you gave the kid your keys, did he give any indication of where he was headed?"

Swift shook his head. "He said he had to get away for a while. He didn't specify how long, but he asked me not to drop him from the program, which tells me he planned on coming back."

"Maybe."

"If he was on the run for killing his father, why would he bother to stop by my office and beg me not to drop him from the program?"

"I don't know. I know that people under extreme stress don't always behave logically. You've been a mentor to this kid. Maybe he wanted to see you one last time, but he couldn't tell you the truth about why."

Despite Swift's instant repudiation of the idea, it sounded logical. Plausible. Swift knew only too well how it felt to grab desperately for your old life, for any kind of stability, when the ground started to give way beneath you.

Max's voice jarred him from his reflections. "So Corelli gave you no idea of where he was going?"

"I thought he was going to the bungalow. Just from the way he reacted when I gave him the keys, I was sure I'd find him there."

"Are you sure he *hadn't* been there?"

"Well, I'm not a forensics expert, but the place felt— smelled, looked—like it hadn't been opened since I was there during the summer. Everything was exactly as I'd left it. Only dustier."

Max rubbed his bearded chin meditatively. "So you have absolutely no idea of where Corelli would go if he was in trouble?"

"No. I'd hope that he'd come to me. Which he did. Beyond that...no. I don't know anything about his personal life."

Max made a sound, not exactly a snort, that indicated this was no surprise. What did that mean? Was it supposed to be commentary on Swift's social interactions? Because how was

Max in a position to judge? He had only permitted Swift into a small corner of his own life.

"Can you think of anything that might be useful?" Max asked. Meaning that so far nothing Swift had had to say was useful? That was probably true. At least from Max's perspective.

"I've told you everything I know."

Max inclined his head, accepting that much. "I don't need to tell you—hopefully—that if Corelli *does* get in touch with you, you need to contact me immediately."

"No." Max's eyes narrowed and Swift added quickly, "No, you don't have to tell me. I know I fucked up."

"Yep. You got that right."

Swift opened his mouth to apologize again, but all at once he was tired of it. He was sorry, sincerely sorry, but he wasn't going to grovel. In fact, he was starting to get irritated. His eyes met Max's, and he saw that Max was reading him quite accurately, lip cynically curling.

Neither spoke for a few strange moments.

"Why *did* you do it?" Max sounded curious. "Why did you keep it from me? Aside from the fact that you were breaking the law, you had to know it wasn't going to...end well between us."

That cool *end well between us* knotted Swift's stomach, doused his flare of rebellion. If he'd realized at the time that he was ending things between himself and Max, then of course he'd have handled matters differently. Didn't it go without saying? He'd never intended or wanted to lose Max. Maybe he'd been naïve enough to think that whatever was between them was strong enough to survive—no. The fact was, he just hadn't thought far enough ahead. He'd acted on impulse. And his efforts to fix his mistake had failed. It was that simple.

Max was still waiting for an answer. Swift said, "It wasn't a conscious decision."

"Really? Were you unconscious at the time?"

"You know what I mean."

"No, I don't. I can't begin to understand what the hell went through your head. I've tried."

"I know it doesn't count for much now, but I wanted to spare him—"

Max's face changed instantly. "Christ. Spare *me*," he interrupted. "He played you, Swift. You don't get that yet, do you? You still think, what? He's innocent and hiding from the real killer or some other bullshit story?"

Swift deserved that. He was probably wasting his breath, but he tried anyway. "No. I don't know. Will you just listen to me, Max? Can't you give me that much?"

Max pressed his lips against whatever it was he dearly wanted to say. He waited. Pointedly.

Swift knew that set, stubborn line of Max's jaw. He wasn't going to change Max's mind. Not about Tad and not about himself. He tried anyway. He had to. It was too important not to try, however unflattering to himself the truth was. "I'd been clean for two years when I got word my...dad had died. I heard it on the nightly news. That's one reason I'm not big on television."

Max's expression altered infinitesimally. He started to speak, but Swift rushed ahead. He needed to say it while he still had the guts.

"I'm not saying I wouldn't have relapsed anyway. They were a rough two years. Every day was a struggle. But what I *can* tell you is finding out the way I did sent me into a tailspin." He didn't want to think about that time. The time when his entire world had been reduced to the rat-bag motel he was living in and his regular trips to the local crackhouse, when all he had lived for was the next line of coke, when he would have done *anything*...and all too frequently had.

"The only reason I'm alive today is I had enough people who cared whether I lived or died to step in and...save me from myself."

"I know you identify with this kid. But so what?" There was no sympathy, no understanding in Max's face.

Swift's forehead wrinkled. "So...what?"

"What did you think you were doing here? Sponsoring the Bingers and Bedbugs Boys Club?"

It was the disgust in Max's face that was hard to take. Max despised junkies. He made no secret of it, though he'd tempered his comments once he'd learned Swift's history.

"I was trying to help. I didn't know—"

"No you didn't. You knew nothing about anything, but you still stuck your oar in. You ever hear the saying 'the road to hell is paved with good intentions', Teach?"

There was no bending, no softening. What had Swift hoped? He met Max's hazel gaze. "Yeah. I've heard that one." He turned away.

He could feel Max watching him, though the other man was silent now. Outside the classroom door, Swift listened to the racket of kids moving through the halls, laughing, calling out despite the fact that other classes were in session.

All at once he was very tired, amped-out, although the letdown here had nothing to do with artificial stimulants.

Max said finally, "All right. You thought that your breaking the news to him would make some difference." His tone wasn't exactly kind, but Swift could tell Max was making an effort not to be cruel again. "But Corelli already knew his old man was dead because he killed him."

That glimmer of protest within Swift sparked back to life. He faced Max. "Maybe you're right. But whatever happened to presumed innocent?"

"Whatever happened to coming forward and explaining your side of it to the police?"

"Kind of a waste when the police chief already has his mind made up."

Max's gaze flattened. "I hope this kid is worth everything you put on the line for him."

Swift gave a tired laugh. "Me too."

Max stood motionless for a moment. Then, "I'll be in touch."

It was not a promise of sweet things to come.

It was hard, very hard, to be on the outside—and Swift was most definitely on the outside now. In fact, looking at the uncompromising set of Max's shoulders, the ramrod-straight line of his back, it was difficult to believe they'd ever laughed together, let alone made love. Not that it had been love for Max. Swift was not convinced it had been love for him either, although he had clearly felt more than the other man.

A lot more.

He busied himself erasing the boards so he didn't have to watch Max walk away.

Chapter Six

You are the first mate of the ocean-research vessel North Star. Your ship has been chartered by the United Nations for a very special mission. Your mission is to travel to the Antarctic to investigate the mysterious disappearance of a satellite during a routine check of ice-melt levels.

Speaking of ice-melt levels... Swift shook the ice in his glass and glanced around for the waitress.

She caught his eye across the brick-wall divider. He indicated another round for the table, and she smiled acknowledgment.

Swift relaxed. He liked this place. Liked the dark wood paneling and the gleaming brass fixtures, liked the faded prints of early Stone Coast. Bean's Tavern had been around since the Revolutionary War. The food was good, the beer was better. He and Max came here sometimes for dinner. It was busy but somehow private thanks to the smoky lighting and high-back leather booths.

Once a month Swift hosted dinner in the tavern's back room for the six or seven graduates and current students of the Lighthouse program who lived locally. Lighthouse was a low-residency program which meant that the majority of students spent fourteen days on campus at the beginning of each semester participating in intensive workshops before returning to their regular work lives. During the rest of the semester the Lighthouse students corresponded online or by phone with their faculty advisor. The idea behind low-res programs was to offer MFAs for those unable to interrupt their lives and current careers to earn their degree.

Now and then another Lighthouse faculty advisor joined them at these monthly get-togethers, but the idea was Swift's and he paid for the dinners out of his own pocket. He received monthly living expenses from a strictly monitored trust fund left to him by his father.

The money had been a sore spot for a few years. Swift had petitioned legally once for control and had been denied. That had been a humiliating process. There was nothing like having friends, family and your health-care professionals go on the record that they did not believe you were (or ever would be) competent to manage your own business affairs—and then having a judge agree. It had been equally humiliating when his trust-fund checks were cut in half the minute he'd begun to earn a steady salary teaching. The official explanation was simple and blunt. While his trustees approved of his decision to work, too much money would present a temptation to him.

In other words, it was only a matter of time before his next relapse, and they all knew it.

Anger over that had helped him through a few difficult nights. And, in fact, the amount of his trust-fund checks had gradually increased to an additional couple of hundred dollars each month, so someone somewhere had apparently determined that Swift deserved an atta boy after six years of being clean and sober. He would never be allowed control of his trust fund—that had been spelled out to him in court—but for the most part he no longer cared. The extra money was nice, but he lived comfortably within his means, and he was proud that the only time he'd had to ask his trustees for an additional

69

dime was for the down payment on his house.

"Sometimes I wonder if poetry is even relevant in our modern society," someone down the table was saying.

It was a popular refrain at these dinners. Swift had long ago decided it was a rhetorical question and no longer engaged in the debate. Maybe he *was* getting old.

He tossed off the final mouthful of drink. He restricted himself to one scotch on the rocks on these evenings. He was actually a little shy in intimate gatherings and the alcohol helped, though he knew better than to start relying on that. Tonight he was dealing with his various stresses by allowing himself a second drink. It was getting to be a habit after each run-in with Max, and even as he ordered it, he wondered if he was starting the first slippery steps down a very steep path. But the nagging, restless *want* had stuck with him all day, and it was starting to scare him.

Three, four hours. That was the longest the craving should persist. Especially this long into his recovery. But as it didn't seem to be fading, he needed to numb it. Despite what the professionals advised, he believed that tonight his best option was alcohol. Coping strategies came in all sizes and shapes. He liked this little band of students and ex-students, but he didn't want to be here. Nor did he want to hear anything more about Tad Corelli this evening, but not surprisingly it was the main topic of dinner conversation.

"I always thought it was a mistake to include an undergrad student in the program." Shannon Cokely tapped a finger on the rim of her wineglass to get the waitress's attention.

Shannon was tall and pale and intense. She taught at the University of Maine, and she wrote poetry as sharp and painful as broken razors.

"I know," Swift said. "You've never failed to mention it."

That was the alcohol loosening his tongue, but he did resent the fact that Shannon had taken her objections over his head to the administration. Swift had triumphed, but it had adversely affected his feelings for Shannon, and he had declined to be her faculty advisor when she'd requested him. She had tried to go over his head that time too, and had again been overruled. Now she restrained herself to regular letters of complaint to Swift about the program, about the other instructors and students, and about Swift himself.

Shannon flushed at his comment, but the others laughed, so maybe Swift hadn't sounded as acidic as he felt. Or maybe he did. Shannon wasn't terribly well-liked for all her talent.

"It looks like he's given Nerine the boost she needed," George Steinberg observed. George worked on the *Stone Coast Signal*. "She's ahead of Bill McNeill in the polls now. They were neck and neck just a few days ago."

"I thought she was pulling out of the race." Swift didn't follow local politics any more than he followed local sports, but he did remember the various conversations he'd overheard that day.

"She'd be a fool to pull out now," Shannon said.

George replied, "She's not pulling out."

"Does Tad have a girlfriend?" Swift asked suddenly.

The others looked surprised at the change of topic, and then doubtful. That was part of the problem including someone Tad's age in the program. That he was as gifted as anyone else in the program was never in dispute, but despite the maturity of his work, he didn't have much else in common with his Lighthouse peers.

"Probably," George said. "The police ought to know." His dark gaze met Swift's, and Swift realized that his relationship with Max was not the secret he generally assumed it was.

"For some reason the police aren't communicating with me."

Everyone laughed as though he'd made a joke, but if so, the joke was on Swift.

"*Is* the kid the only suspect?" George asked, and Swift remembered belatedly that George was first and foremost a reporter.

"I don't know. I thought one of the waiters was a suspect."

"Antonio Lascola," George concurred. "He threatened Mario after Mario fired him, but it turned out he had an alibi."

"What was his alibi?"

"He was with his girlfriend."

"You're kidding. Even *I* know that's a lame alibi."

George shrugged. "Maybe. Lascola's green-card status depends on being employed, so he did have motive, but unfortunately it sounds like Tad had more. A number of people confirmed that he threatened to kill Corelli."

Cory Kolodinsky drawled, "My kids threaten to kill me once a week," and everyone laughed again.

Swift said, "But that's just it. He's a kid. Kids say things like that."

"And sometimes they mean them." Shannon looked up as the waitress arrived with the tray of drinks. "I didn't want this," she objected as the waitress set a fresh drink before her.

"What would you like?"

"Something else."

The waitress failed to conceal her flash of irritation. "What something else?"

"Just forget it." Shannon's lip trembled before she hid it behind her drink.

The waitress shrugged and moved on to the next person.

"Order anything you like," Swift told Shannon.

She glared at him over the rim of her glass.

Never, if he lived to be a hundred, would Swift understand women. Starting with his own mother and moving right down the line to Shannon.

"It's no secret Corelli used to knock Tad around," someone else commented.

"Is that speculation or is that fact?" Swift asked as the waitress set his drink before him.

"That's fact." George reached for his own drink. "Both Nerine Corelli and the kid's own mother corroborate that. Mario had a mighty nasty temper."

"Here's something I don't understand," Swift said. "Corelli was killed out at Wolfe Neck, right? How does that make sense? What was he doing out there?"

"That's where the body was found," George informed him. "Nobody but the police know if that's where Corelli was actually killed. The body could have been moved."

Oh. Duh. Swift picked his glass up and sipped his scotch. Safe to say he was not cut out for the amateur-sleuth business. He never read mysteries if he could help it, and when he did read them, he always got them wrong.

One of the other students spoke up. "Corelli supposedly had mob connections, didn't he? That was always one of the rumors."

"*Mob* connections? If that's the case, I can't see why the cops have focused on Tad." The others were gazing at Swift curiously, and he realized once again that they imagined he had insider knowledge.

"Probably because he ran," Shannon said shortly. "It's not

exactly a sign of innocence."

"It's not automatically a sign of guilt."

No one responded to that, and Swift knew it was more to do with not arguing with the guy picking up the dinner tab than agreement.

"Maybe the boy's on drugs again," Cory suggested. There was an intensely awkward silence. "That is..." She cleared her throat.

That's what happened when your own messy prior drug habit was a matter of public record.

Swift smiled at her. He liked Cory. She was even one of his neighbors on Orson Island. Among other things, she worked in the tiny library. "Maybe. I never saw a sign of it, but...maybe."

After that, the conversation flowed into different channels, and Tad's problems were forgotten in the face of the more pressing concern of what to order for dessert.

There was one Ariel—and only one Ariel—enrolled at CBC. Ariel Rhoem, a sophomore majoring in biochemistry. The poet and the biochemist? It felt unlikely, but Swift took Rhoem's info down and thanked the clerk in Admissions for her help.

Unless Tad had left the county, he had to be somewhere close by. Swift was convinced of it. As of Tuesday morning, he had still not been found, and there was talk of bringing in the state police whether Police Chief Prescott wanted them or not.

Knowing how Max would feel about surrendering his investigation to another agency, Swift winced. If not for his own inadvertent interference, Tad would be safely in Max's custody.

Or maybe not. Since Tad had not headed out to Orson Island as planned, there was no guarantee that he'd have been located as easily as Max believed. Swift would have liked to point that out to Max, but regardless of where Tad was, Swift's silence on the matter was perceived by Max as a betrayal.

It was hard to argue with that. Even if Max had still been talking to him.

On his way out of the Admissions office, he left a message on Ariel's cell phone and another with the RA in charge of her dorm. He didn't mention why he wished to see her, but he was pretty sure she'd respond. Not many students blithely ignored a summons from an instructor, even if the instructor wasn't their own.

On his lunch break, Swift drove over to Nerine Corelli's campaign headquarters in the community center on Center Street. It was Election Day, and inside the building was a beehive of activities overlooked by giant black-and-white posters of a serenely smiling Nerine Corelli.

All this for the mayorship of a village that didn't even show on most maps of Maine?

Swift said no thanks to a *Racing to Excellence* button and politely declined invitations to sign up for knocking on doors, phoning voters, putting up signs or monitoring polls. Wasn't it too late for all that anyway?

No, no! Every vote counted. Right up to the minute the polls closed.

Eventually he found his way to the candidate herself. Nerine sat at a long table covered with pamphlets and handouts. She was typing at a laptop.

Nerine greeted Swift politely, though her enthusiasm waned when she realized he was neither reporter nor voter. She was strikingly attractive, probably mid-forties though no one would have openly challenged her if she claimed younger. She wore her dark hair in a stylish updo vaguely reminiscent of Sarah

Palin. Her eyes were a dramatic shade of blue behind trendy glasses.

"Coffee?" she invited, leading Swift to another table with tall urns for coffee and tea, and baskets full of bagels.

"Thanks." Swift accepted a paper cup of what looked like tar and dosed it liberally with sugar and Cremora.

"I'm brain dead without at least three cups." Nerine leaned against the wall of a cubicle plastered with her photos and blew on her scalding coffee. "What exactly can I do for you, Professor?"

Swift started to speak, but was interrupted by a chirpy young woman who hurried up to ask Nerine about balloons.

Balloons? That sounded as though victory was being anticipated.

Nerine approved the balloons, and the young woman bustled away. Nerine fastened her blue-gray gaze on Swift once more. "I'm sorry. Where were we?"

It occurred to Swift that he was handling this all wrong. Not that he could be expected to know the right way to question someone, but he was probably worse at it than most people. "I don't think I offered you my condolences."

Nerine gave a weary laugh. "That's all right. This will sound terrible, but I can't let myself deal with it. Not until after the election. Mario and I both sacrificed so that I could get this far. As cold-blooded as I'm sure it seems, I'm not about to give up now. Especially when—" She stopped.

Especially when what? When she was so close to winning?

"I don't know whether the police mentioned to you that Tad came to see me Thursday afternoon."

Her immaculately shaped eyebrows rose. "When?"

When? There was that word again. A pragmatic soul, the

Widow Corelli. She sliced right through the usual questions.

"Around four o'clock. He stopped by to ask me not to drop him from the Lighthouse program, but I think now, looking back, he was asking for more. I think he was asking for my help."

"Your...help? Your help with what?"

"I don't know, but I feel guilty that I wasn't able to do more."

Her gaze seemed to challenge him. "Did Tad tell you he'd killed Mario?"

"No. Definitely not. If he had—"

"Tad didn't kill Mario," Nerine cut in brusquely. "At least, I'd be flabbergasted to learn otherwise. I don't care what the police say. Tad's a screwup, but he's no killer."

"Did you tell the police that?"

"Of course!"

"What did they say?"

"They said it was natural that I would feel that way." Nerine's expression was disgusted as she sipped her coffee.

"Do you think it's possible Tad's staying with friends?"

"Friends?" Nerine sounded like it was an unfamiliar concept.

"It seems like what a kid would do."

"Do you have children?"

"No."

"I didn't think so."

That didn't seem quite fair. Swift figured after six years of teaching he was probably as much an expert on young adults as Nerine Corelli. He said only, "Do you know who Tad's close to?"

She shook her head briskly. "Tad and Hodge Williams have been buddies since grade school."

"Can you think of anyone else?"

"No."

They were interrupted by another volunteer, this one round and matronly, wanting to know about sandwiches.

Nerine made short work of the sandwich issue. Corelli's Ristorante would be supplying foot-long spicy Italian sandwiches, coffee and tea. And, if victory was announced that evening, there would be champagne.

"Do you think you'll win?" Swift asked when they were alone again.

"I usually win." It was said with a supreme calm confidence that Swift rather envied. Nerine smiled politely. "Was there anything else you wanted, Professor? As you can see, things are hectic today."

"I do see that. I just wondered if you have a-a theory about anyone who would have wanted your husband...out of the way?" Swift felt like an idiot asking, but how else did people find out this stuff? Nerine seemed so sure Tad wasn't guilty.

"If *I* have a theory?"

"Er, yes."

Nerine gazed at him in disbelief. "You're damn right I have a theory. The person the police should be investigating is Bill McNeill."

"You mean the mayor?"

"I mean my political opponent. Bill and Mario nearly came to blows two days before Mario was killed. I always knew McNeill would do anything to be reelected, and now I have my proof."

"*Do* you have proof?"

She looked at Swift like he was a moron. "If I had *proof*, the police wouldn't still be wasting the taxpayer's money chasing after Tad. It's a figure of speech."

"Right," said Swift, who knew a thing or two about figures of speech. "Do you know what your husband and McNeill fought over?"

"No."

That was clearly not true—and she clearly didn't care that Swift knew it.

"Do you have any idea where Tad might go if he was in trouble?"

"Apparently he went to *you*." She didn't actually *say* that was Tad's first mistake.

"Yes. I offered to let him stay at a bungalow I own out on Orson Island, but he never showed up. Does he have a girlfriend?"

"A girl? There was usually a girl. I didn't keep track of them."

Swift thought about asking whether she'd ever heard of anyone named Ariel Rhoem, but decided it was wiser to keep his cards—well, his sole card—close to his vest.

Nerine was still talking. "To be honest, Tad and I weren't close. Or maybe you know that. He was already in his teens when I came along, and he always resented me. His mother didn't take the divorce well, and she basically brainwashed him."

"Was that the reason Tad and his father didn't get along?"

"Do fathers and teenaged sons *ever* get along?"

Swift had adored his father, but they'd had their disagreements. Fierce and, occasionally, bitter disagreements. That was one of the things that he would have fixed if he could

79

go back in time. He wanted every single one of them back, the minutes wasted on arguing over things he no longer even remembered. "Sometimes."

"Not in my experience. I know the police want to build something out of Tad's last quarrel with Mario, but they fought all the time. They fought constantly. It meant nothing. Two hot-blooded Italian men under the same roof." She shook her head. "I'd have been worried if they *hadn't* argued."

"I understood that Tad had substance-abuse problems."

She was silent. "That's true," she admitted at last.

"Do you think he was using again?"

She sighed. "I think it's possible. Tad's a bright boy—well, you know that—but he has issues." She glanced away as someone waved their way. "You'll have to excuse me. I have a million things to attend to."

Swift nodded.

Nerine started to walk away but she stopped. "Even if Tad *is* doing drugs again, I don't believe he killed Mario. The man to look at is Bill McNeill."

Chapter Seven

You are a poor young farmer in seventh-century China. Day after day you toil with your humble parents in the fields. One day a horde of barbarians descend upon your village and take you captive.

And at this point that would be a big relief because if one more kid stops by to ask whether he missed anything "important" when he skipped class this morning, you're probably going to commit some rape and pillage of your own.

Swift recognized the irritability born of too much caffeine and missed lunch. Tonight he needed to make sure he ate properly and got a good night's rest. But first he had the rest of the day to get through and the usual mountain of papers.

One thing he did not plan on doing was take Nerine Corelli's advice to seek out Bill McNeill. McNeill would have no idea where Tad was, and finding Tad was Swift's only concern. Solving Corelli's murder was for the police.

Someone tapped on the frame of his office door. Swift looked up.

A slim brown-haired girl in a pink parka and Ugg boots regarded him uncertainly. "Professor Swift?"

Swift nodded.

"You wanted to see me?"

"Did I?"

"I'm Ariel Rhoem."

"Oh. I did. You're right." Swift rose, and Ariel looked uneasy at what probably appeared to be abnormal eagerness. "Come in, please. You can close the door."

She closed the door. "What's this about? I'm not a lit major."

"Please. Sit down."

She obeyed slowly, lowering her satchel and taking the chair across from him. She tucked a strand of hair behind her ear and eyed him warily.

"I'm trying to get in touch with Tad."

Sometimes Swift's unconventional social skills served him surprisingly well. Ariel's mouth dropped open. She didn't speak although her lips moved. She didn't ask who Tad was, she didn't deny knowing him.

The unexpected triumph spurred Swift on. "He's in big trouble, Ariel. I think I can help him, but to do that I need to talk to him."

"I don't know where he is."

Swift didn't believe that feeble protest for one moment. "You must have some idea. Even if you don't know for sure."

Ariel gave a little stubborn shake of her head as though she didn't trust words. She watched Swift with worried green eyes.

"Did Tad tell you he came to see me? Why didn't he go to the island?"

Her head moved, but she stilled before she gave herself away with an actual nod. Swift was now certain she knew where Tad was. The important thing was to avoid scaring her lest she alarm Tad into running further.

"I don't know where he is," she repeated stubbornly.

"I haven't told the police about you."

Her eyes went wider still. "Everyone knows you and Chief Prescott are..."

Swift shook his head. "I wouldn't betray a confidence."

"It doesn't matter. I don't know where he is."

"Ariel. Please."

Ariel bit her lip. She burst out, "But Tad didn't do it."

"Then he has to come forward and say so."

"No one will believe him. *You* don't believe him."

"I don't know if he did it or not. To be honest...I don't care."

She looked almost comically shocked. Kids were so endearingly conservative—despite what they believed.

"Anyway, I don't think he killed his father," Swift said mostly to reassure her.

"That's not what the police think."

"Partly that's because of the way Tad is handling this. He's doing the worst possible thing by running away."

"You don't have all the facts." She did sound like a science major then.

"No one has all the facts. How can we when Tad hasn't told his side of the story?"

She stared unhappily down at her satchel. "When he tells his side of the story, it's just going to make it worse."

Swift thought that over. "I'm not sure what that means. If Tad didn't kill his father—"

She raised her head. "Mario used to slap him around. Everyone knows that. Everyone knows Tad said he'd kill him if he ever did it again."

"*Did* Mario hit him again?"

She shook her head, but Swift wasn't sure if that indicated

refusal to answer or an actual negative. "Okay, but if Tad *didn't—*"

"Motive, means, opportunity..." She ticked each word off on her fingers like a detective on one of those horrible shows where half the story was a grisly autopsy.

"Did he kill his father or not?"

She blinked at the sharpness of Swift's tone. "*No.*"

"Then he has to come forward and deal with this. Believe me, I know what I'm talking about. Unless Tad's planning to spend the rest of his life on the run, and he's obviously not since he's still hanging around here." Swift overrode her instinctive denial. "Of course he's still hanging around. He's still in contact with you. He asked me not to drop him from class. I don't know where he is, but he's not far away."

She gave another one of those stubborn shakes of her head.

"Listen to me. Tad *has* to talk to someone. He might as well start by talking to me."

"Why should he?"

"Because I'm on his side. He ought to know that by now." Swift slid forward a slip of paper with his cell phone number on it.

"He won't call you."

"I think he's smarter than that."

Ariel's throat moved.

"At least let him decide for himself. You must have some way of getting in touch with him."

"No."

"Yes. He wrote a poem to you. I don't mean dedicated. I mean he wrote a poem to and *about* you. Unless things have changed a lot since I was Tad's age, he's got feelings for you. If he's in contact with anyone, he's in contact with you."

"I keep telling you he's n—"

Swift rode right over her. "Tell him that I want to help. Tell him I'll do everything possible for him, but he's got to get in touch with me."

She shook her head.

Swift sat back and regarded her. Ariel gazed at him with defiance. Swift said coolly, "Tell him I'll give him until noon tomorrow, but after that I'll tell Chief Prescott about you."

Ariel flushed angrily. "I knew it. You're just like everyone else."

Swift gave a short laugh. "No, I'm really not."

No sooner did Ariel's angry footsteps disappear down the hallway than Dottie rapped on the half-open door.

Swift looked up inquiringly.

Dottie said curtly, "Doctor Koltz wants to see you as soon as possible."

"*Me*?" Swift sounded as guilty as one of his own students. Dr. Koltz was the college president. He was a large, cordial man, but Swift always had the impression that he made Koltz uncomfortable. If so, the feeling was mutual.

"Immediately." Dottie's satisfaction heightened Swift's instinctive unease.

"All right. I'm on my way." Swift rose. Dottie continued to stand in the doorway watching him as though he was liable to slip out the window. "Was there something else?"

"No." Dottie smiled tightly and withdrew.

Swift glanced uncertainly around his office, grabbed his coat and headed off to the administration offices.

The rain had stopped and the sun was out. All the world looked dazzlingly bright and newly minted. Green grass, red brick, white stone, blue skies. Primary and intense. The light was different in autumn. Vibrant and alive in a way unique to the fall. Swift used to spend a lot of time and words trying to describe that particular luminosity. There were such good words: lambency, incandescence, effulgence—although effulgence had always sounded like an illness. Yet all those wonderful, clever words couldn't capture the shimmer of golden light on red leaves and white birch.

Maybe that was why Swift had stopped writing.

What was the use when you couldn't capture...well, whatever it was he'd hoped to capture.

Maybe it would be different if he were to try now. But to try now would be almost like starting from scratch. He couldn't imagine it. In fact, the very idea of trying again made sweat break out over his back in a kind of emotional heat rash.

No. It was too late. That bridge lay in ashes behind him. Better to keep moving and never look back. Safer.

Swift reached the administration offices and went inside. As always he was struck by the hush in these buildings. The administration offices were the quietest on campus. That was a mandate sent down from on high. Dr. Koltz liked quiet and order.

Swift checked in with Maggie Nalley, the president's administrative assistant, and he was shown into Dr. Koltz's office immediately.

His nervousness increased at the sight of Koltz on his feet, hands behind his back as he gazed thoughtfully out at the pristine green lawns of the campus.

Glancing around at Swift's entrance, Koltz cleared his throat and said with forced heartiness, "Swift. Sit down please."

Koltz was a big man. Tall and broad shouldered with thick, iron gray hair. He looked like the football player he'd once been. He also looked the distinguished and successful master of academia—a role he enjoyed very much if his frequent appearance in the pages of the *Stone Coast Signal's* society column was anything to go by.

As Swift complied, Koltz moved to his own throne-sized chair and sat down behind the desk. He smiled like a man determined to put the best face on an unpleasant task.

"I'm afraid some disturbing news has come to my attention."

"To do with me?" Swift asked, startled. It had to be disturbing news if Koltz was dispensing with the awkward chitchat. Had Max changed his mind and gone to Koltz? It didn't seem like something Max would do.

"I had a call a little while ago from Nerine Corelli." Koltz waited. What he was waiting for, Swift wasn't sure. He seemed faintly disappointed when Swift said nothing.

"Mrs. Corelli said she had reason to believe that you know the whereabouts of her son, Tad, and that you're misguidedly helping the boy evade justice."

"*What?*"

Koltz winced at Swift's yelp. He made a patting gesture with his large, manicured hand as though trying to push the sound of Swift's voice back into an invisible box. "I don't have to tell you how serious this situation is."

"I don't have to tell you how ludicrous it is."

Koltz frowned. That wasn't how instructors were supposed to address His Eminence. "Did you not tell Mrs. Corelli this afternoon that Tad had been in contact with you?"

"Yes, but—"

Koltz shook his head disapprovingly and, with the regretful air of someone about to sign a death warrant, reached for a pen. What the hell was going on?

Swift spoke up. "That was Thursday. Five days ago, and Chief Prescott knows all about it. I have no idea where Tad is now." Not for lack of trying, but it was a relief to be able to deny culpability with conviction.

Koltz's curling eyebrows drew together. "Chief Prescott knows about this?"

"Of course," Swift said staunchly. He was probably presuming a lot on the part of Max, but despite everything that had happened between them he trusted Max to back him up. At least in a skirmish with this blowhard. Max had never been in the Koltz camp. Something to do with campus parking violations.

"You're saying you have no idea where the boy is?"

"If I did know, I'd be urging Tad to give himself up."

Koltz made a noncommittal noise. Finally he said, "That isn't what Mrs. Corelli believes."

"I can't help what Mrs. Corelli believes. I don't know where she came up with her crazy theory. I went to her hoping *she* might know where Tad was."

That must have been the wrong thing to say because Koltz's mouth turned down. "You seem to take a great personal interest in the Corelli boy. You insisted that he be included in the Lighthouse program and now this. May I ask exactly what your relationship is?"

"May you—? No, you may not."

Koltz's eyebrows beetled. "I beg your pardon?"

And so you should, Swift thought, but he had enough restraint not to say it. "I'm Corelli's instructor and his mentor in the Lighthouse program. And I hope to some extent he regards me as a friend, but there's no relationship there. Not the way you seem to mean."

"We have a strict non-fraternization policy at CBC as regards to students and their instructors."

"I should hope so."

Koltz stared at Swift with grim suspicion, and Swift gathered that Koltz had been all set to pursue a course of action and now that the course appeared closed, he was at a loss as how to proceed. Was disappointed, in fact.

Koltz said uncomfortably, "Your, er, orientation is not a secret."

"No, it's not."

Another stalemate.

Koltz cleared his throat. "And if I phone Chief Prescott, he's going to confirm that you reported your meeting with the Corelli boy?"

Swift could feel himself losing color. Something was going on here that he didn't understand. Until this instant he hadn't realized that Koltz was hoping for a reason to get rid of him. In fact, gazing into Koltz's hard eyes, Swift realized that Koltz actively disliked him.

That was both disconcerting and confusing, but even more confusing was Nerine Corelli going to the college with whatever her complaint was. She hadn't seemed angry or suspicious during their brief meeting, so what had changed?

Becoming aware that Koltz was still waiting for a reply, Swift said stiffly, "If you feel it's necessary to check up on me."

"This isn't personal, Professor Swift," Koltz said quickly. "Faculty members hold a position of trust and must be above reproach. We all know you've had some issues in the past.

Happily nothing that we're aware of during your tenure at CBC, but I have to think of the college when someone—let alone the mayor—makes an accusation like this."

"I wasn't aware she was the mayor yet."

Koltz's cheeks went slightly pink. "Mrs. Corelli is the mother, er, stepmother of the missing student, that's the real point."

No, it wasn't, but whatever the real point was, Swift couldn't figure it out. He said tersely, "Be my guest. Call Max."

Koltz's eyes flickered at the deliberate reminder of Swift's own political alliances. He said in his normal hearty way, "I have no doubt Chief Prescott will confirm everything you say, and we'll be able to put this unpleasantness behind us."

Swift took that as his cue to escape and rose.

He almost didn't have the nerve to go back to his office knowing that Dottie would be waiting and watching, hoping for a sign that he'd been suspended or at the least suitably reprimanded.

Swift knew he wasn't everyone's cup of poison, but it did shake him to recognize he was actively disliked in certain quarters. He had always considered his presence a fairly insignificant blip on the CBC radar.

When he reached Chamberlain Hall, he quietly opened the side entrance and sneaked down the empty hall to his office. This was likely what Tad had done the afternoon he'd waited for Swift. Granted, Tad was a kid, and Swift was a grown man who probably ought to show a little more backbone.

To his relief no students waited for him. He let himself in his office, closed the door and locked it. He left the light off and sat down behind his desk, resting his face in his hands. For a few minutes his thoughts were a chaotic jumble of resentment, fear and bewilderment.

What if Max didn't back him to Dr. Koltz? What if he gave Koltz the whole, unvarnished story? Swift's stomach did a flop like a dying fish, and he reached for the phone on his desk. He realized the red message light was blinking.

He stared. More bad news? He wasn't sure he could deal with it.

Instead he dialed Max's cell. His heart pounded so hard with an irrational mix of nerves and worry it was almost hard to breathe. Maybe the years of drug abuse were about to catch up and he was going into cardiac arrest.

"Prescott," Max answered abruptly. If he'd seen the number flash up, he didn't sound particularly thrilled to hear from his former fuck buddy. Swift's anxiety shot up another degree.

"Max..." The word cracked. Swift froze. He didn't trust his voice. It was like having vertigo and being stuck on a ladder— unable to climb up and unable to crawl down.

"Still here," Max said after an agonizing second or two.

Swift put his hand to his throat and squeezed, trying to control the threatened shake. "Did...Dr. Koltz...call?"

"That blubber-ass windbag," Max said. "I just got off the phone with him."

Koltz must have snatched the phone up the instant the door closed behind Swift.

Into Swift's strangled silence, Max clipped out, "Don't worry. I corroborated your story."

Swift squeezed the muscles in his throat so hard it hurt. "Thanks."

Max said dryly, "Don't mention it. And I do mean that." He disconnected.

Swift listened to the buzz of dial tone. It sounded...final. At last he replaced the handset, remembered the blinking light and pressed the button for voice mail.

"Swift, my dear," Bernard's slightly fuzzy voice greeted him.

Swift's first thought was that somehow his involvement in the Corelli case had made its way into the national news, but Bernard's next words cleared that up. "I wondered if you'd had time to think over what we discussed the other day."

There was even a little pause as though Bernard was waiting for Swift's response.

"The last thing anyone wants is to put undue pressure on you, but it's been almost seven years, after all. Time, surely, to have come to terms with...everything."

Another pause before Bernard's voice returned with that confessional note.

"You must remember what Richard Rosen said? *The poem is the point at which our strength gave out.* It's time to go back and *look*, my dear. You're strong enough to face it now."

Swift quietly pressed the receiver button.

Chapter Eight

You've arrived at the banks of the Yanayacu River to join a medical expedition in the Amazon jungle, but base camp is completely deserted. Your colleagues have been lured into the shadowy jungle by the eerie music of a mysterious flute. Now you are alone with only strange Incan hieroglyphics left in the sand to guide you.

If you choose to spend time translating the message in the sand, turn to page 36.

If you choose to follow the eerie music of the flute, turn to page 97.

Or, given your luck, maybe you better stay safely at base camp and hope the rescue team shows up before you starve to death or have to resort to eating palm grubs.

Swift stared down at his plate. Arugula salad with grilled mushrooms and goat cheese. It just as well might have been palm grubs, given his appetite.

The doorbell rang, startling him out of his dismal thoughts.

He shoved his chair back and went down the steps and across the long polished wood floor to answer the door. As he passed the angel in the alcove, his pulse picked up—he didn't want to examine *why* too carefully.

Whoever he was expecting, it was not the plump but

attractive middle-aged woman on his doorstep. She was quite short, with salt-and-pepper curls. She wore a leather jacket and jeans.

"Yes?" Swift waited to hear a sales pitch for a church he did not belong to and never would—belonging being a two-way street.

"Are you Professor Swift?"

The wise answer was probably *who wants to know?* Swift settled for a cautious nod.

"I'm Cora Corelli. Tad's mom."

"Oh?" Swift said still more cautiously. Given the unpredictable result of his chat with Nerine Corelli, he was on his guard.

"I wanted to thank you for what you did for my son."

"I didn't actually do anything. I'd have been glad to help, but—"

"Tad's been framed," Cora blurted.

Swift's shoulders slumped. There wasn't any getting around this. "Would you like to come in?" He already knew the answer.

Cora nodded and crossed the threshold. Inside the entrance hall, she gazed about at the long, open rooms, the martial angel guarding its alcove, the soaring ceiling, the paintings. Her stare traveled up the narrow staircase to the loft with the decorative iron railing and the winged bronze.

"Jesus, Mary and Joseph. What kind of place is this?"

Was that rhetorical?

"I guess it suits you." Cora's dark eyes met his. "Is your mother still living, Professor Swift?"

"Yes." Swift was still trying to decide if there was an insult in her comment about his living space. It was probably not a compliment.

"Are you close to her?"

"No."

Understatement of the decade. Even before she had publicly blamed the worry and anguish over Swift for contributing to Norris's failing health, Marion Gilbert Swift had washed her hands of her "terminally troubled" only child. Forget Dr. Spock. Marion had been into the Three Strikes school of parenting.

Not that Swift really blamed her. He'd have washed his hands of himself too—in fact, he'd tried pretty determinedly to do just that.

"That's wrong," Cora said. "A mother is a boy's best friend."

Swift just managed to keep from saying *I thought it was a dog.*

"My son is everything to me."

"He's lucky," Swift said politely. Personally, he thought she sounded like a nut. *Come hither, my dear Hamlet, sit by me.* Surely she was something other than just Tad's mom? Swift tried to picture her twenty years younger. She was so utterly different from Nerine Corelli. A couple of decades ago she'd probably been a cute armful, but temperamentally she'd have been much the same—in fact, she'd probably mellowed. People usually did.

"Someone is trying to frame my son."

"So you said. Why do you think that?"

"It's obvious."

It wasn't obvious to Swift. "You think your ex-husband was killed just to frame Tad?"

"No, no. Of course not." Cora turned away, slowly walking the circumference of the main room, studying the paintings and objets d'art littering the shelves. "But whoever killed Mario deliberately tried to implicate Tad."

"That seems unlikely," Swift said, watching her examine a tall bronze finial that someone had sent him after *BS* had been published. It was supposed to be from the Chapelle Saint-Blaise-des-Simples in Milly-la-Forêt where Jean Cocteau was buried. People had done things like that, back in the day. Sent him gifts. Wrote him deeply personal letters about how his words touched their lives. "The most damaging piece of evidence was the fact that Tad ran, and how could anyone know he'd do that?"

"Whose side are you on?" Cora demanded, turning to him. Tears filled her eyes and brimmed over.

"I want to help Tad however I can," Swift said honestly. "I just don't follow how or why you think he was framed."

"Because whoever killed Mario knew that Tad would be the first person the police suspected."

Was that how it worked? Swift had a vague memory of Max once saying that the first person to look at in a homicide was the spouse. Or maybe ex-spouse? Were children equally suspect? What a voracious world it was.

"Let me tell you about Mario. The divorce was his idea. I didn't want it. I'm a good Catholic. I don't believe you end your marriage because you get tired of waking up next to the same person every morning for fifteen years."

Swift opened his mouth, but Cora drove right past. "Nerine was a *hostess* in our *family* restaurant."

"I didn't realize."

"That's right. A hostess." Never had a simple job description sounded so sleazy. "And not as young as she acts, either. But he decides he's going to marry her. Okay. I can't stop him. But then he decides that a boy needs to be with his father, and he insists that he's going to have custody of Tad."

"Wasn't Tad old enough to have a say?"

"Yes. But Judge Vecchio was a golfing buddy of my husband. So was Dave Luthor, my lawyer. Mario knows—knew—everybody in this town. So *I* got cheated on, and *I* got partial custody."

It sounded to Swift like she had cause for grievance. Of course there were two sides to every story.

"Do you have any idea of where Tad is?"

Cora shook her head. "I thought you might. I need to see him. He needs me now."

Why did everyone think Swift knew where Tad was? And why the hell couldn't Tad have confirmed everyone's assumptions and just gone to Orson Island?

"I don't know where he is."

"I heard you do. Nerine says you do."

So the first and second Mrs. Corelli were now on speaking terms? The divorce had clearly not been amicable. Nerine had seemed to concur on that point. But maybe time had healed some wounds. Or maybe Mario's death made the old injuries irrelevant.

Swift replied, "I don't know where Nerine got that. I went to see her in the hope that *she* knew where he was."

"She wouldn't know. Tad wouldn't go to her for help. He's *my* son."

Here be dragons. "Right. Well, she seemed to agree with that. Do you have any idea of where Tad might go?"

Cora shook her head.

"Do you know where his girlfriend—?"

"Tad doesn't have a girlfriend," Cora interrupted.

"Oh." Swift considered this, deemed it wise to let it ride.

"What about friends? I know he used to hang with Hodge Williams and Denny Jensen."

"Denny, yes. Hodge and Tad grew up together. But they don't have so much in common anymore. Not after Tad quit the football team. Most boys think poetry is for pansies." Meeting Swift's eyes, she shrugged. "Sorry, but that's the way it is."

"I know some people think that way," Swift replied, because what purpose would be served by debating it with her? This was a woman who believed she was her son's best friend. "Are they still close enough that Tad would go to Hodge or Denny for help?"

"I already asked Hodge. He said Tad went to you."

Now they were getting somewhere, because how could Hodge know that Tad had been to see Swift unless Tad had told him? It wasn't something Max was likely to spread around.

"Mario wanted Tad in his life. What was Tad's relationship like with his father?"

"Mario was not a good father."

Swift's father had been one of the best. Unfortunately he hadn't realized it at the time. But maybe that was true of most kids. "Is that what Tad thought?"

"Of course that's what Tad thought. It's what everyone thought. Mario was never there when Tad needed him. Not there in body and not there in spirit. And when he got mad, watch out." Cora wiped at the tears, smearing her mascara.

"He hit Tad?"

"Tad, me, anyone who pissed him off."

"Did you ever file assault charges?"

"No!" Cora sounded like Swift had said something ridiculous. She looked at the black smudges on her fingers. "Can I use your little girl's room? I need to freshen up."

Swift raised an eyebrow, restrained himself, pointed. "It's the white door around the pillar there."

Cora thanked him and disappeared between the carved pillars.

Swift went into the kitchen and put the teakettle on. He felt certain he was going to need a quiet, calm cuppa once the ex-Mrs. Corelli departed.

She rejoined him in a few minutes, her boots clicking as she marched up the steps to the kitchen. "This is a church, isn't it?"

"It was, once upon a time."

"That's a sin, isn't it?"

"It's deconsecrated."

She looked unconvinced. "It doesn't seem right. You've got an oil painting of St. George."

"The building is just stone and wood now. Like any old building." Okay, perhaps that was an exaggeration. Swift did feel there was a special serenity between these walls. Sanctuary. It was a good thing.

Cora shook her head, still dissatisfied.

Swift thought it best to change the subject. "Who do *you* think killed your ex-husband?"

"That bitch Nerine."

Okay. Some wounds never healed. This one was still wet and gaping.

"Why do you say that?"

"It's obvious."

"If it was obvious, wouldn't the police focus on her rather than Tad?"

"Mario was *shot*. Tad hates guns. Nerine is president of

Women on Target."

"What's Women on Target?"

"The women's branch of our local Rod & Gun Club."

That was interesting, but not something Max was likely to have overlooked. "It's interesting that you accuse Nerine. She suggested Bill McNeill."

Cora broke into slightly hysterical laughter. "That's great. I love it."

"I guess I don't get the joke."

"Her blaming McNeill. Not that he couldn't have done it. He's as big a scumbag as Mario was."

"She said McNeill and your ex-husband had a fight just a few days before Mario was killed."

"Did she tell you *why* they fought?"

Swift shook his head.

"They fought because McNeill was having an affair with the slut."

"How do you know that?"

Cora looked at him as though he was simple. "*Everyone* knows that."

It had been a very long day. Another long day. After Cora finally left, Swift wandered restlessly around the house. It felt tight and confined. Like being in a box. He went out to the backyard, the former church garden, and sat on a stone bench for a few minutes gazing up at the mercilessly bright stars in the black sky. The night air smelled of freshly dug earth, dead leaves, and, more distantly, wood smoke.

He tried to focus on what his senses reported, tried to use

the cold and the silence to clear his mind, but that internal itch was crawling through him again. He *wanted*.

He wanted all the things he couldn't have.

He thought about Cora and Tad and then for the first time in a long time he thought about his own mother. Every so often, usually when he least expected it, he forgot his anger and animosity and just...missed her.

The back of his eyes burned. He blamed it on Bernard and the reminder of those fucking poems. He should have ripped them to pieces.

He couldn't afford this. Couldn't afford to start thinking about these things. He would never be strong enough to face these memories. The memory of his mother blaming him for his father's death, telling him he should be locked up so he could never hurt anyone again.

Just as he'd done his best to fulfill her wish that he become a poet, he had done his best to fulfill her wish that he'd never been born.

And yet it was Marion who had paid for the expensive treatments that had saved his life and his mind. The same Marion who had fought to have him permanently committed to a mental hospital, and when that failed, fought successfully to keep him from gaining control of his inheritance.

Not that he blamed her for the last two. He didn't really blame her for any of it. But he couldn't forgive her either.

And thinking about this did no one any good. Least of all him.

Swift went back inside the house, went into his office and pulled out the blue rigid paper box with its melancholy images of clouds and autumn leaves. He stroked the laminated lid absently.

Who had collected his poems after his final spectacular crash and burn? Bernard or someone hired by his mother? Someone had come to that motel where he'd been living and gathered up the few belongings he hadn't pawned or sold for coke, gathered up these poems scribbled on scrap pieces of paper with the rest of the detritus, saved it all on the off chance he survived.

Or perhaps the belief that he wouldn't.

Swift's thumb stroked the lip of the lid. *Were* they any good? Were they coherent? Were they even legible?

Did it matter?

He picked the box up and put it back in the drawer. He slid the drawer closed.

Bernard's timing was off. A week or so ago Swift might have felt strong enough to face whatever was in this pretty box, but not tonight. Not now. Tonight he felt about as fragile as he had in six years of staying clean and sober.

And whatever was in this box might be the final straw, might be just enough to tip those delicately balanced scales the wrong way.

In which case he might as well take the ferry to Orson Island this very night. That was the promise he'd made himself. That if he ever started using again, he'd spare himself and everyone else the party and just take a long walk into the ocean.

He rose, turned out the lights and left the office.

Exhaustion that was partly lack of sleep and partly the strain of fighting the longing for things that were bad for him had Swift in bed and reading by nine thirty.

He fell asleep somewhere between images of birds breathed into the sky and banging cymbals of sunlight. In his dream he was writing and the words came quickly, one at a time, in flashing, fierce scissor snips...

Swift jolted awake what felt like mere minutes later. His eyes flew open. The loft lights were still on and someone was downstairs banging hard on the front door. He sat up, knocking aside the book lying open on his chest, shoving the blankets aside, grabbing for a sweatshirt and pulling it on as he stumbled barefoot downstairs.

He turned on the porch light, looked blearily through the spyhole, jumping back as the door shook once more beneath an impatient fist.

Max.

Swift slid the bolt back and wrenched the door open.

Max wore jeans and his usual off-duty sheepskin jacket. He regarded Swift for a long moment. His breath silvered in the night air as he said, "Can I come in?"

"Yeah. Of course." Swift raked the hair out of his face, stepping back.

Max didn't move. "You should know this is official business."

Swift's heart sank. "Okay."

"Are you still giving me permission to enter?"

Swift drew a sharp breath. Shit. This was bad. He'd heard Max talk about this enough to know that Max wanted in to search but didn't have a warrant. Did Max really think he was so far gone he'd hide Tad in his own home? Nerves made his voice raw. "Yeah, I'm giving you permission to enter. Knock yourself out."

Max's nod was grim. "Okay." He stepped inside and shut the door. He stared at Swift. Swift stared back.

When Max didn't move, Swift said, "Well?"

"We received an anonymous tip this evening that you've got a stash of cocaine here."

Chapter Nine

You are a former poet, former drug addict, former...

You are...

You're totally fucked.

And he hadn't seen it coming. Swift reached out to steady himself and nearly knocked the small painting of a whitewashed barn off the wall. "*What?*"

Max continued that cold, unblinking appraisal.

"You're telling me this is a...a drug bust?"

"I'm telling you—" Max stopped. Maybe it was harder for him than it looked.

"What?"

"I'm telling you that I'm going to search this place because I wouldn't be doing my job if I didn't."

"There's nothing here. You *know* there's nothing here." Swift's teeth started to chatter. That was partly cold—he had no resistance to it—and partly nerves. Either way it was mortifying. He gritted his jaw to try and conceal it.

"If you want someone else to do it, I can get a cruiser over here in three minutes. I won't be able to keep this under wraps," Max added, "but if there's anything here, I won't be keeping it under wraps anyway."

Swift's legs gave out and he sat down on the carved pew

beneath the still-swaying painting. Max watched him, waiting for an answer—and what the hell answer was there to this?

He found words at last, croaking out, "Do what you want."

Max nodded once, curtly, and walked away toward the kitchen area. Did he think Swift was keeping coke in a special canister next to the sugar and flour? He heard the squeak of the first cupboard door and rested his face in his hands.

He didn't watch. He couldn't watch. It was like seeing Max dismantle his dreams, one cupboard, one drawer at a time. Clearly Max had a lot of practice at this. He moved briskly, knowledgably. He searched the fridge, the freezer, the pantry. He finished with the kitchen and moved on to the main room, ignoring Swift who still sat unmoving, head in his hands.

Max searched the backs of shelves and beneath cushions, he searched potted plants and even behind stacks of CDs. He moved on to the downstairs bath.

Swift pressed the heels of his hands hard against his eyes and listened to the ceramic scrape of the toilet-tank lid being lifted. What was the big deal? He'd been through lots of things worse than this. Lots of things a lot more humiliating than having a cop, even an ex-boyfriend cop, search his home for drugs.

A few seconds later Max appeared before Swift. He held out a clear plastic baggie. It was about a quarter full of white powder.

Swift opened his mouth. Closed it. He stared at Max. He stared at the bag of white powder. Licked his lips.

Was he dreaming? It felt like a dream. A nightmare. It felt far away and absolutely impossible. The horror of it prickled across his scalp and down his spine.

Part of the horror was certainly the discovery of an illegal substance in his home. A greater part of the horror was the instinctive and fierce desire that shuddered through his nervous system at the sight of that bag of white powder hanging right there within his reach. It had been there all the time, all evening while he was wanting it, needing it, aching for it. And it had been right there. His for the taking.

And he *would* have taken it. The realization terrified him.

Max said with no inflection in his deep voice, "Anything to say?"

Swift tore his gaze from the bag of powder. He said desperately, through the click of his teeth, "I'm not using, Max. I'm clean. I swear to God. I *swear* it." Riiiight. How many times had Max heard that one? Swift no doubt even looked like someone crashing down hard. Even his nose was starting to run. He wiped at it surreptitiously.

"Yeah? A drug test will prove it one way or the other."

It took a couple of seconds for the words to filter through the panic. A drug test. *Of course.* Swift slumped back in relief, unconsciously hugging himself. "That's right. Jesus, that's right."

Max gave a short, harsh laugh. He shoved the bag into his jacket pocket. Swift watched it vanish, couldn't tear his gaze from it. He could feel Max staring at him.

Swift made himself meet Max's eyes.

"Hell," Max muttered.

Unexpectedly, he lowered himself to the pew beside Swift, and it said something for Max's effect on him that Swift actually forgot about the bag of coke for a few seconds.

Max expelled a long, weary breath and leaned back, his shoulder brushing Swift's. He regarded the dark open beams overhead. "You, my friend, are in one hell of a mess."

"Someone planted that coke."

"Do you think I don't know that?" Max turned his head. His hazel eyes met Swift's. "Forget everything else, you'd have to be a moron to stash this in your guest bathroom."

As compliments went, it wasn't much, but Swift would take it. "Someone's trying to frame me." There was a lot of that going around.

"Why?"

"I don't know."

"You better start thinking."

"It doesn't make sense. There's no reason—"

"Who've you pissed off lately?"

Swift shook his head.

"Flunk anyone? Drop anyone? Reject any poetry submissions?" Max wasn't kidding. There was no smile in his eyes, his tone was even.

Swift considered the day he'd had, from his brief meeting with Nerine Corelli—a meeting she'd apparently taken serious offense to—to his visit from Cora Corelli. All things considered, not one of his most productive days, but this...this was just out there.

"I don't know, but I know who had to have planted the blow."

"Yeah? Who?"

"Cora Corelli was here this evening. She used the bathroom."

"Cora Corelli?" Max was doubtful. "The first wife?"

"Yes. It has to be her. No one else has been here."

Max said nothing for a long time, seeming to think it over. "The anonymous caller was female. Why would Cora Corelli want you arrested?"

Swift shook his head. "I don't know. She came by this evening because—she said—she was sure that I must know where Tad is."

Max's face hardened. "If you *do* know—"

"I don't. Max. I don't know. Do you honestly think after what's happened—?"

"All right."

It cut Swift off but only for a second or two. He admitted, "I did try asking around today."

Max's eyes narrowed. "What do you mean you tried asking around?"

"Just that. I was thinking. Tad can't have gone far, and if I could talk to him, I could persuade him to give himself up before anyone else gets hurt."

Max was shaking his head. "Stay out of it, Swift. I realize you're trying to help, but tonight should have made it clear you're out of your depth."

Yeah, no kidding. Swift darkly considered the bitter truth of that. "But it's not like I'm...I'm trying to play detective. I'm not trying to solve a murder. I don't give a damn who killed Mario Corelli. I just care about Tad. And all I've done to that end is ask a couple of people if they knew where Tad was. Next thing I know, Nerine Corelli is lodging a complaint with that bastard Koltz—"

"What?"

Swift filled Max in on the entire circumstances of his meetings with both Nerine and Dr. Koltz.

"That's weird," Max commented, sounding more like his old self. "You didn't say anything that might have given the impression you knew where Tad was?"

"I'm sure I didn't. The whole reason for talking to her was

to see if she knew where he was. I don't know if it's some kind of homophobic subtext to all this. Koltz practically accused me of abusing my position to..." It was too painful to complete the thought.

Max got the message anyway. "You're shitting me."

"And then Cora said a couple of things. Not directed at me. At least I didn't think so at the time. Poetry being for pansies."

Max grunted. He probably agreed with the sentiment. "What brought that up?"

"The fact that these days Tad doesn't seem to have anything in common with his old buddies. Then again she didn't know Tad had a—" He stopped too late.

"That Tad had a what?"

He was going to be in trouble again if he admitted to Max that he'd kept quiet about discovering Tad had a girlfriend no one apparently knew about. But this was how he'd got in trouble before—keeping things from Max.

Swift said vaguely, "I think Tad might have been in love."

"With you?"

Swift's jaw dropped at the weird expression on Max's face. He stuttered, "No, not with me. Are you saying *you* think I'd have sexual relations with a student?"

He must have looked sufficiently distressed—and hurt—because Max said instantly, "No. I do not. But kids do sometimes develop obsessions for their professors."

"There was nothing like that. Tad's straight."

"Maybe not. Maybe his family knows something you don't."

"I think I'm in a better position to judge *that*."

"I'm not so sure. You can be..."

"I can be what?"

"Oblivious."

"Oblivious?"

"You pretty much live in your own world, Swift." It was blunt but void of aggression. It was simply an observation.

Swift frowned. "Everyone does."

"Not quite to the extent that you do."

Swift mulled this over. Patently, Max wasn't trying to hurt or offend, and maybe there was some truth to what he said. Swift wasn't sure. If Max thought Swift was self-absorbed now, he should have seen him a decade ago. By that old standard, Swift was practically Mother Theresa.

He conceded, "I don't think Tad is gay and I don't think Tad has a thing for me, but maybe—well, no maybe about it— something is going on here I don't understand. Either someone doesn't want Tad found or someone wants to make sure I keep a safe distance from him. Or maybe both."

"I want you to keep a safe distance from him too," Max said. "No more asking questions, no more poking around."

"I was...trying to repair some of the damage I did."

Max's gaze didn't waver. After a very long moment he said, "I know."

Swift looked away. He nodded.

Max rose at last. "I have to go log this stuff into evidence."

Swift looked up at him. "Are you—you're not going to arrest me?"

Max shook his head.

"No drug test?"

"No."

He could have cried with relief. Happily he didn't. The night had been humiliating enough. "How are you going to explain that?"

"I'm the police chief. I don't have to explain anything. If the voters don't like the way I do my job, they can vote me out in two years."

Was it that cut-and-dried? But things *were* cut-and-dried for Max. Cut-and-dried, black and white. In some ways that was part of what Swift liked about Max. It was also what scared him about Max.

Max continued to look at him in that unfathomable way. Swift searched for something to say, some neutral topic. "Who won today's election for mayor?"

"No one yet. They're doing a recount. It's too close to call."

Swift nodded. He watched Max walk to the door. His heart sank. What did he want? He should just be grateful Max was letting him off the hook. But he was greedy. He wanted more. Even if it was just a few minutes of Max sitting beside him.

Max opened the door. He glanced back at Swift, hesitated.

Swift waited. With one thing and the other, it had been a long day.

Max said gruffly, "I could...come back. Later."

Swift stood. "I thought you—I thought we were finished."

Max's mouth curled in self-mockery. "So did I. We were. For the first two hours after I threw you out of my office. But..."

"But?"

Max shrugged. "It's not over. For me."

It was more—a lot more—than he had expected. "It's not over for me."

Max met him halfway. The sweetness of that first kiss made Swift's eyes sting. He'd been so sure this was lost forever. So sure he was alone in his longing and regret. But Max was holding him as though Swift were safely returned from some long and perilous journey. And so it felt to Swift. He hugged Max tight.

"I'm so goddamned *sorry*," he muttered into Max's neck. "I never meant to hurt you. Never you."

Max's words reverberated against his face. "Me too."

Swift raised his head, and Max reached up to stroke the hair back from Swift's forehead. "I know what you were saying yesterday. I think I understand."

"Thanks." It felt inadequate. He'd never expected understanding from Max. Forgiveness if he was very lucky. Understanding? He wasn't even sure he deserved it.

Max let him go reluctantly. "I have to go. I'll be back though."

Swift nodded.

Max said with impatient affection, "And for God's sake put some socks on. Your feet are blue."

Swift smiled for what felt like the first time in a long time. He nodded again.

After Max left, Swift stood gripping the doorknob, feeling the warmth from Max's hand against his skin.

Swift tried to wait up. He showered and shaved, changed into clean sweatpants and replaced the sheets on the bed with fresh ones. He considered what he would cook if Max arrived hungry. The fridge and freezer were always packed with food. He could probably cook Max almost anything he wanted.

But after the first hour he began to worry that Max wouldn't come back. Maybe he'd be too tired. Maybe he'd have an accident on the way. Or maybe, when Max had time to reflect, he'd decide that on second thought being involved with Swift was more trouble than it was worth.

Swift should have taken the time to explain his actions. All he'd done was offer excuses and say sorry, and no one knew better than Swift how little sorry really meant. He should have reassured Max that he understood where he'd gone wrong and that he'd learned his lesson.

Anxiety triggered need and the nagging want was made worse by the knowledge of the cocaine that had been hidden downstairs. What if more cocaine was stashed somewhere in the house? Max had stopped looking after he found the baggie in the bathroom. Maybe there was more.

Swift battled and won the desire to start looking, but the fight drained him. He was overtired, stressed and craving. He knew from experience the best way to deal with this was to sleep. So he climbed back into the freshly made bed and stared up at the tall arched window with its blue-and-red stained-glass panels.

It would be nice to believe in something like God. To believe some higher power with a greater purpose was concealed behind the violence and chaos. Once upon a time Swift had believed in poetry. Now he wasn't sure he even believed in that.

People did terrible things to each other—and half the time they did it by accident.

He sifted over the day's events. None of that had been accident. Why had Nerine turned him in to Dr. Koltz? Why did Dr. Koltz dislike him so much? Why did Dottie dislike him so much? Why had Cora planted the coke? What kind of a threat did he present that so many people wanted him...gone?

It couldn't all be related to Tad. Dottie hated all addicts on general principle. He could safely discount her antagonism. Dr. Koltz? Maybe he thought Swift was overpaid for what he contributed to the university. Maybe he was homophobic. But Nerine? And Cora was definitely on Tad's side, so why try to torpedo the only other ally Tad had?

It didn't make sense.

Swift remembered Mario Corelli from the times he and Max had eaten at Mario's restaurant. Corelli was a handsome, personable man. He'd reminded Swift a little of Dean Martin, charming and boozy but rougher around the edges. Corelli joked with the guests and watched his staff like a hawk. Everything had to be perfect from the breadsticks to the fresh flowers.

Even if he did slap his son around now and then or borrow a little from the mob once in a while, odds were he wasn't an evil man. True evil was pretty rare in Swift's opinion. Corelli had been well liked locally and two women had loved him. Even his son probably loved him. Almost certainly loved him. It wasn't easy to stop loving your parents.

That didn't mean Tad hadn't killed his father. Swift had loved his own father but his actions had contributed to his death. He knew Norris was in poor health, knew Norris worried about him.

He closed his eyes. It wouldn't help anyone to think of this now. He couldn't deal with anything else tonight. To calm himself he mentally recited Wilfred J. Funk's 1932 list of "most beautiful words". It was his mantra on restless nights like these. Ten words that generally knocked him unconscious if he concentrated on them hard enough.

Melody.

Golden.

Chimes.

Luminous.

Mist.

Tranquil.

Murmuring.

Lullaby.

Hush.

Dawn...

Swift opened his eyes. The tableside lamp was off. Max stood beside the bed. He stripped in quick, efficient moves, the muscular planes of his body silvered by moonlight.

Pulling back the blankets, he slid into bed, reaching for Swift.

The mattress dipped and they rolled into each other's arms. Max's body radiated warmth. His scent, musky and male, in pleasant contrast to the crisp smell of the sheets, found Swift.

They kissed, but it was a gentle kiss and there was no urgency. They were tired and they were...healing. They had time. And time was the most beautiful word of all.

Chapter Ten

Your space pod has crash landed on the lush and beautiful planet of Timblaine. The planet seems very much like Earth with one exception: the purple and yellow skies have been invaded by deadly space dragons. The fierce dragons threaten Timblaine's very existence. You agree to join in the battle to save Timblaine— but there are things your alien hosts have not told you.

So what else was new?

By Wednesday midmorning, news was circulating that Nerine Corelli had won the race for mayor. Was that the sympathy vote or did people really believe Nerine would do the best job?

Swift had not voted. He didn't keep abreast of civic affairs, so maybe Max was right. Maybe he did live in his own little world. For years it had taken all Swift's strength and will to keep that little world clean and intact. If he was self-absorbed— and he probably was—it wasn't in the normal way. It was his intention to keep from hurting or disappointing anyone again. Whether the living or the dead. To do that...took a hell of a lot of focus. But if he managed to make it look casual, like he was just an ordinary egotistical prick, that was an achievement.

He wondered who Max had voted for.

When he thought of Max he could feel his face creasing into a self-conscious smile. He couldn't help it. It was such a relief that they were back to...whatever they were.

Despite everything else going on, the thought of Max was like an anchor. Swift had never thought of happiness as a weight before, but that's what it felt like. Something solid and real to steady him, ground him. Not that you could—or should—rely on another person to keep you straight, but it helped that there was someone to whom his staying straight mattered.

After his first lecture of the morning, he returned to his office and sat watching the clock and waiting for Ariel to call with news of Tad.

"Bernard Frost," Dottie announced over the intercom.

Swift swore under his breath. He pressed the button and picked up.

"Swift," Bernard replied cheerfully to his terse greeting. "I should apologize. I didn't realize you weren't allowed personal calls."

"I'm...huh?" Swift said intelligently.

"That dragon lady who answers your switchboard seems to think you're getting too many personal phone calls."

Swift spared *switchboard* an amused thought before Bernard's comment fully registered. "Is that what she said?"

"Words to that effect. I'm sorry if I—"

"No. Of course not. Not at all. I'm allowed to—I'm an instructor here for God's sake." Swift was nearly stuttering his anger. Anger and bewilderment. Who did Dottie think she was? She was a glorified office clerk. How fucking dare she imply anything? How fucking dare she *think* anything?

He missed Bernard's next few remarks as he dealt with his righteous indignation. He probably got fewer personal phone calls than anyone in the entire English department. Not that

that was the point, but it added to his ire. And his worry. Because if Dottie was being so flagrantly disrespectful, maybe she knew something Swift didn't.

Like his days were numbered at CBC?

He realized that Bernard was still talking. "What? I'm sorry?"

"The poems for the *Blue Knife* collection. Have you thought about what we discussed the other day?"

"Are you serious?" Tension over the situation with Dottie—among other things—edged Swift's voice.

"I don't mean to nag, but you did say you'd think it over, my dear."

"I meant one day in the future. Not this week. This week is not good. I'm not sure this year is good."

"Ah."

Ah? WTF? No way had Bernard called to ask about those damned poems, because one thing he wasn't was obtuse.

Swift forced his voice to evenness. "What's going on, Bernard?"

The pause sent a prickle of unease down his spine. "I told you I spoke to Marion."

"Yes. So?" He closed his eyes and waited rigidly for word of disaster or terminal illness.

Bernard said only, mildly, "She was...er, asking after you."

Swift's eyes opened. "Was she." It was not a question because that was a question he wouldn't allow himself to ask.

"I think she would like..."

Swift stubbornly held to his own silence as Bernard's voice trailed away.

Bernard said abruptly, "If this thing is ever going to be

healed, you'll have to make a...a reciprocal gesture, you know."

Now that was almost funny. Swift couldn't quite keep the quiver out of his voice. "Reciprocal gesture? What gesture is she supposed to have made? Telling you she remembers I'm still alive?"

"You're not the only one who lost him, Swift."

He wasn't expecting the kick in the guts. The burn that closed his throat and blurred his vision caught him off-guard. Words were beyond him, and it was a struggle to get the next breath without making a betraying sound. He could only cling to his silence and hope it sounded like strength and hardness rather than the childish desire to give in to a grief there was no healing.

"She and Ralph are good for each other, but it's not the same. Nothing could be. She still...I'm not saying she was in the right. I'm only saying she did the best she could given...who she is."

Swift struggled to keep that tidal wave of emotion pushed down in his chest.

"Are you there?"

"Yes."

"You must realize by now that some of the things she did were done to protect you when the, er, outlook was not hopeful."

"Yes." Those weren't the things he couldn't forgive, and Bernard had to know it.

"She's...sorry. She misses you. She just doesn't know how to say it."

The words tore out. He couldn't stop them. "Tell her to write a poem." Swift disconnected with a shaking hand.

The phone call from Bernard rattled him enough that he forgot all about Ariel and the ultimatum he'd given her until he was in front of his Reading Poems seminar and his cell phone rang.

Max.

There were the usual titters as he excused himself and stepped into the hall. Through the door he could hear Susan Hogg's prim, muffled voice reading Pablo Neruda's "Tonight I Can Write the Saddest Lines".

I no longer love her, that's certain, but maybe I love her.

Love is so short, forgetting is so long.

Max was brisk. "Cora Corelli denies planting the bag of coke in your john."

"I don't care what she says. She did it. She had to have."

"She swears up and down on a pantheon of saints that she wouldn't know where to get such a thing. And, to be honest, I believe her."

"Max, I swear to you—"

"Stop."

Swift stopped.

"Listen to me. We need to have this straight between us. I don't think you're using again. I know you're not. I'd have noticed."

Because he was a cop or because he watched Swift for the signs he'd slipped back into using? Or both? The thought of either bothered him.

"Then unless *you* planted it, Cora wanted to get me arrested."

He said it to provoke, and he could tell by Max's tone that he'd succeeded. "Do you want a serious answer to that?"

"No. But no one else has been out to the house. Cora used the bathroom to, her words, freshen up. And if it's true that Tad is using again, maybe she found the coke in his things."

"Yeah, well about that. I went back through Tad's rap sheet and as far as I can find, his drug habit seems to amount to nothing more than smoking weed a couple of times with some other punks."

"Oh." Swift was ashamed that he felt even the least disappointment that Tad's drug problem should turn out to be so trivial, but there was no denying he'd felt an added kinship believing Tad had fought free of serious addiction. Not that he wished that—God forbid—on anyone, but every success story reassured him that his own victory was real and lasting.

"Cora Corelli is an average suburban housewife. I believe her when she says she has no idea where to get hard drugs."

"All right," Swift said wearily.

"This is someone who knows your history and has a certain amount of street knowledge."

"All anyone has to do to know my history is to Google me. It's all there." Swift added, "Or they can look back through *my* rap sheet."

Max ignored the challenge. "So...next move. I want you to call a security company."

"Come on, I'm not going to flip out and turn the place into a damned fortress."

"Listen, Swift. Someone planted coke in your home and then made an anonymous phone call to the police. Someone wanted you arrested. Possibly to put you out of action, possibly to destroy you. That much is for sure. If the Corelli woman is telling the truth—and I think she is—then someone deliberately set you up."

"I already know that."

"So unless you think your cleaning lady has it in for you, someone broke in."

"The cleaning lady comes today. And I think I'd have noticed if someone had broken in."

"I don't. Not unless they broke in while you happened to be standing there."

"Well, *you'd* have noticed, right?" Swift said a little waspishly.

"I wasn't looking for a break-in. I wasn't expecting to find *anything,* to be honest. I figured some asshole wanted you harassed for giving him a bad grade on a test. But as far as breaking into your place—it wouldn't be hard to do. A determined kindergartener could get in without a lot of trouble. You don't have any kind of security system, and the locks on the windows and doors are mostly original. I've told you before you need to invest in some hardware."

"Please don't say I told you so. I'm having enough of a bad day."

"Then I won't say it. But here's Jerry King's number. He's good and he's reasonably priced."

Max quoted the number, and Swift typed it into his BlackBerry.

"Got it," Swift said.

"Okay." Max's tone changed. "Are you really having a bad day?"

Swift's heart lifted. "It had a great start, which helps."

He could hear the smile in Max's voice. "Yeah. It did. If I can get away, should I come by tonight?"

Swift was smiling too as he said, "Yes. Try."

Max rang off and Swift checked his messages again. Still no

word from Ariel. It was now one thirty. It looked like she was calling his bluff.

It wasn't a bluff though. Swift wasn't about to risk his newly rescued relationship with Max again. There was only so much you could do to help people. The rest of it they had to figure out for themselves.

On his lunch break Swift called his old therapist, Dr. Bayer, only to discover that the Safe Horizon clinic was closed. Dr. Bayer had moved her practice to Florida. Two years ago.

Maybe someday that would be funny. Right now? Not so much.

Once Swift had seen Dr. Bayer a court-mandated three times a week, but gradually it had tapered down to once a week, then once a month and then, finally, nothing. It had been three years since his last session, but it had reassured him to know Bayer was there if he got into trouble.

He was not in trouble now—at least he didn't think so—but it would have been good to talk to someone who already knew him and his history. The idea of starting over with a new doctor felt humiliating. Was that silly? Probably. It was certainly illogical. But he'd been proud of the fact that he had moved beyond needing counseling and therapy. To seek out a new therapist, to admit that he still might need help, was too much like acknowledging failure.

Besides, if it got back to Dr. Koltz and the college administration that he was once more seeking counseling for drug addiction, it might send up warning flares. They were liable to assume he was using once more or losing the battle to stay clean.

Anyway, it had been just a thought. He didn't really need to talk to Bayer or anyone else. It would have been comforting, perhaps, but he was all right. He'd been all right for six years now. He wasn't going to do something stupid. Whatever he was feeling right now was simply the result of stress. And there were other ways to cope.

Even so it did feel like being in the middle of a complicated high-wire act and looking down to realize they'd removed the safety nets.

The day passed with no word from Ariel, and when his classes were finished for the afternoon, Swift walked across campus to her dorm. This, judging by the flutter of excitement in the henhouse, turned out to be a miscalculation. Professors did not casually visit students in their dorms and have it go unnoticed.

On top of that, Ariel wasn't in her room and hadn't been back to the dorm in the last twenty-four hours, so it was a wasted trip. Swift trudged back to his office. A red light was blinking on his desk phone, but when he listened to the message, it was Shannon Cokely bitching yet again about Tess Allison's failures as an MFA advisor and asking to come see him.

Shannon would not be happy until she had Swift as her advisor, and yet as far as he could tell, Shannon thoroughly disliked him. She certainly would dislike him if she had him for her advisor, he thought grimly. Maybe he should give her what she wanted.

Dismissing Shannon from his thoughts, he returned to the problem of Tad.

He had been excusing the possibility of Tad committing patricide as a tragic consequence of his drug addiction, but it turned out Tad didn't have a serious drug addiction—though

125

seemingly news to his stepmother. Then again, a lot of people lumped all drug use together, like an occasional joint was the same as sitting around doing coke every night until the sun came up.

No drug habit to feed meant Tad might manage to stay on the run longer. Even so, Swift was convinced that Tad was getting help evading the cops. The boy's face had been plastered on the local TV stations and in the newspaper, so he couldn't be staying in town. He couldn't buy his own groceries. Someone *had* to be helping him.

Swift was betting on Ariel, and if she thought she was going to avoid him by staying away from her dorm, she had another think coming. Swift had a list of contact names and emergency numbers, and he was going to go right down the list until he found someone who could lead him to her.

Nor was he going to give her a heads up with a phone call.

On his way out of Chamberlain Hall, Dottie called to him.

"Professor Swift?"

Swift turned around and walked back to her office. She had her desk angled to make it easy for her to keep tabs on anyone entering the building through the main doors.

"Yes?"

"Are you leaving for the day?"

"Yes." Swift glanced automatically at the clock behind her desk. It was four thirty. No reason that he *shouldn't* be leaving, and no reason for him to feel guilty about leaving. "That's right."

"Is everything all right?"

He didn't trust the bright concern in her yellow-green eyes for one second. "Of course."

She smiled that tight little smile that looked like it hurt. "I just wondered."

He understood that she wanted him to ask *why* so that she could then tell him something guaranteed to upset him. He resisted. "Nope. Everything's fine. Night."

"All those phone calls today," Dottie persisted. "We were all a little concerned."

Don't bite, Swift warned himself, but Bernard's earlier comments rankled. "Since when do you monitor my phone calls?"

"I hardly have time to *monitor* your phone calls with *my* workload," Dottie said with just the right blend of offended hauteur. "I know *I'd* love to be able to go home just once before five o'clock. We're all aware of your past, Professor, and we do try to be sensitive to that. I'm sorry if it appears to you like we're *monitoring* you."

Great. The story making the rounds tomorrow would be that he was suffering from a persecution complex. Swift looked pointedly at the clock and said, "Thanks for your concern. Seeing how busy you are, I'll let you get back to work."

Dottie's mouth flew open in instinctive protest, but Swift had turned and was already on his way down the hall to the main entrance.

He fumed silently all the way to the parking lot, but by the time he was driving out through the school gates, he had cooled down again.

Dottie had disliked him from the first instant he'd stepped foot on the CBC campus, and now she thought she could needle him with impunity. Well, let her. Sticks and stones, right? People he cared much more for had said a lot worse, and he'd survived that. He could survive Dottie.

He followed the directions he'd jotted down to the Rhoem residence on Sandy Beach Lane.

It was an ordinary residential house on an ordinary

127

residential street. Swift parked by the curb and walked up to the front door. No one answered the doorbell though a dog began to bark in the backyard.

Swift knocked and then rang the doorbell again, but it was clear no one was home.

He turned at the sound of an approaching engine. A black, souped-up monster truck with giant tires roared up to the curb. Both cab doors flew open. Hodge Williams jumped down. He reached up and helped out Ariel.

Denny Jensen sprang down from the driver's side.

The three were halfway up the cement walk before they noticed Swift standing beneath the yellow wooden portico.

Denny stopped, grabbing for Ariel's arm, preparing to run. Hodge's good-natured features fell into unfamiliar hostile lines. He squared his shoulders and started up the path toward Swift.

Chapter Eleven

It's the 23rd century. A blood-sucking vampire has stolen away in the cargo hold of a Starfleet Training Academy spaceship. As the academy's highest ranking recruit, it's your job to capture the vicious alien before it can reach Earth and feast upon the overweight, er, unsuspecting population. But not long after you reach the cargo hold, the space vampire corners you. What should you do?

If you decide to abandon ship and flee to the escape pods, turn to page 12.

If you decide to face the vampire and outwit him, turn to page 96.

How come asking for advice was never an option in those adventures? Knowing when to ask for advice was a sure sign of maturity and wisdom, right? Not that Swift didn't know what advice someone—anyone—would give him. He sure as hell knew what advice Max would give at this minute, and it wouldn't be couched in tactful phrases.

"You've got balls coming here!" Hodge snarled.

Swift stood his ground, although it wasn't easy. He had firsthand knowledge of getting punched in the face, and it was an experience he didn't want to repeat. His nose ached in anticipation, although maybe that was the cold, his nose being rather more delicate than some people's.

Through squinting eyes he saw Ariel grab onto Hodge's arm, saw Denny dart in front of him, planting his hands on Hodge's broad chest.

"Don't be stupid, dude," Denny said. It was like trying to hold back a tank.

"Hodge, wait." That was Ariel, tugging uselessly on his arm. "Hodge!"

"This is *your* fault." Hodge's boyish face was red with anger as he barreled toward Swift.

Swift gathered the rags of his dignity and stepped forward. He had no idea what he could possibly say, so it was a surprise to hear his own reasonable, "Don't be stupid, Williams. You're about to make things a lot worse for everyone involved in this mess."

"Says who?"

Yeah. Well, Hodge wasn't the brightest candle on the birthday cake. Swift said, "Says the guy who'll have you arrested for assault, expelled, and therefore kicked off the football team."

He could see this threat ticking over slowly behind Hodge's eyes. Football was probably the most important thing in the world to Hodge, so it said something for the depth of his friendship with Tad when he snarled, "I don't give a shit," and lunged forward.

Self-preservation overrode dignity. Swift ducked back out of reach as Denny and Ariel grabbed for their companion. "Tad came to me for help!"

"Then you should have helped him."

"I'm *trying* to."

"By turning Ariel over to the cops?"

"Have I turned her over to the cops?" Swift replied,

knocking Hodge's clawing hand away. "Do you *see* the cops here? Or do you see me on my own?"

"Will you cool it, dude?" Denny warned Hodge. "You're going to get us all kicked out."

"If you'd left it alone, Tad wouldn't have taken off again." That was directed at Swift, not Denny. As far as Hodge was concerned there was no one on the doorstep but him and Swift.

Ariel dug her keys out of her backpack. She crammed onto the stoop past Swift and unlocked the front door, pushing it wide. "Come on. We can talk inside. My mom won't be home till tonight."

Swift wasn't sure it was such a great idea to go inside. If these three decided to do something *really* stupid, he'd be in one hell of a mess trying to get away, but standing out on the front porch wasn't a good idea either.

He followed the girl inside, uncomfortably aware of Hodge breathing—literally—down his neck.

They trooped into the den, the kids divesting themselves of hats, jackets and backpacks.

"What do you mean Tad wouldn't have taken off again?" Swift asked, turning to Hodge.

"He's gone," Ariel said. "I told him last night what you told me, and he took off again."

Swift swore. "Where was he staying?"

Three stony faces gazed at him.

Swift gazed back with equal disfavor. "Who the hell do you think you are? The Goonies? Your pal is wanted for murder, and you're all technically accessories. The only way to fix this is for Tad to come in and tell his story. The longer he waits, the worse it is for him *and* for you. Why do you not see this obvious fact?"

"Because it isn't obvious," Denny said calmly.

"Really? What's your take on it?"

"That if Tad gives himself up now the police won't look any further. They'll just arrest Tad and throw away the keys."

"That's ridiculous. In fact, that's the opposite of the truth. Everybody is so focused on finding Tad they're not considering the other possibilities." Swift had no idea if that was true or not, but it struck him more likely than the other theory.

"That's what I told them," Ariel said. "I *told* Tad that."

Swift looked from one face to the other. "Does Tad know who killed his father? Is he protecting someone?"

They looked so utterly and completely blank they could have been brain-wiped by the Narozl Mind Eaters in CYOA #186.

"No," Ariel said. The two boys looked at her.

"It was probably a mob hit," Denny said. "That's what I think."

"A mob hit? You mean like organized crime? The mafia?" Swift had never thought about the mob having a presence in artsy little villages like Stone Coast, but apparently it was perfectly possible.

"The *mafia?*" exclaimed Ariel.

Denny looked sheepish but stubborn. "That's what my old man says. He says the mob is tied into the restaurant business. Corelli was in the restaurant business. And he was Italian." He shrugged. *Ipso facto?*

"I think it was that bitch Nerine," Hodge said.

Both Ariel and Denny started to speak. Hodge talked over them, scowling fiercely at Swift. "She was having an affair with the mayor."

"No way." Denny appeared genuinely shocked at the idea.

Swift had noticed that quaint puritanical streak of young adults toward the sexual behaviors of their elders before. It was sort of touching.

Ariel made another of those aborted moves to speak.

"That's what Tad's mother says." Swift watched Ariel. He had the feeling she knew more than she was letting on.

"She was *not* having an affair with Mr. McNeill," Ariel stated. "I know Tad thought that was true, but my mother works for the mayor's office, so I know it's not. Anyway, Nerine's not the type of person who commits murder."

"Maybe McNeill killed old man Corelli," Denny said. "*If* that's even true."

Ariel insisted, "It's *not* true."

"But that would make more sense, if McNeill wanted to get Corelli out of the way."

"Am I talking to myself here? It's not true."

Hodge said, still challenging Swift, "Has anyone even checked McNeill's alibi? Or Nerine's? Or anybody's but Tad's?"

"I don't know."

This was met with obvious disbelief.

"I *don't* know," Swift repeated. "I'm not part of any investigation. Tad brought me into this when he asked for help and I loaned him the keys to my bungalow on Orson Island. *He* came to *me*. And I'm trying to help him."

"It's your fault he's in trouble to start with."

"How do you work that out?"

"Shut up, Hodge," Denny muttered.

Hodge shook his head, but he shut up.

Swift said, "I don't know what you're talking about."

"I'm talking about queers."

Swift absorbed it, absorbed the ugly, harsh word. The funny thing was Hodge always seemed like such an easygoing, affable kid. The epithet sounded all the worse because of it. Swift said quietly, "I still don't know what you're talking about."

"Leave it *alone*, Hodge," Ariel warned.

Swift left it alone too. He addressed Ariel. "After I spoke to you yesterday, what happened?"

Her eyes shone with dislike. "I called Tad on his cell. I told him what you told me, that if he didn't get in touch with you, you'd turn me in to the cops."

"And?"

"He said he'd call you. That he'd get you to stop." She looked at Hodge. "But when we went out there today, Tad was gone."

"When you went out where?"

Ariel looked at Denny. Denny looked at Hodge. Ariel said, "My grandparents have a cottage at Wolfe Neck. Tad was staying there. Until today when he disappeared."

Swift didn't like the sound of that. "And you don't have any idea of where he went?"

She shook her head.

"Is it possible...?" Two thoughts occurred to him. Both were so awful he hated to give voice to them. The kids regarded him uneasily. Swift chose the lesser of two evils. "Is it possible Tad didn't leave voluntarily?"

It was so quiet he could hear the rumble of the heater on the other side of the paneled wall.

"I'm starting to think anything's possible," Ariel said finally.

Proof of his paranoia, Swift thought they might even try to keep him by force while they figured out what to do next, but when he said he was leaving they simply exchanged looks and watched in silence as he walked out of the living room.

He would have to tell Max, of course. But there was no hurry on that. Tad was long gone again, and Swift was not looking forward to facing Max's ire. He couldn't avoid it permanently, but a few hours wouldn't matter now.

He drove home and cooked lambchops with fennel, which was one of Max's favorite dishes. Of course there was no guarantee Max would be able to drop by, so Swift dutifully ate supper on his own, reading over *Passionate Hearts* and absently blue penciling half of what he read.

At first he was fine, but as the hours slid by without sign of Max, he began to think about the cocaine that had been hidden downstairs. He refused to let himself search the house in case more was stashed somewhere, but he couldn't get it out of his mind, and his mounting frustration and anger made it impossible to concentrate.

Why was this happening now after six years? Okay, maybe only three years where he could say with any real confidence that he believed his addiction was firmly under control. As firmly controlled as such things could ever be.

But three fucking years and now suddenly it was back on his mind every fucking second.

The unfairness of it made him furious. It scared him.

And the more he worried about it, the more he wanted to comfort himself chemically.

A Cocaine Anonymous group met in Portland. Maybe that was the answer? Maybe returning to a more structured recovery program until he was steady again? It didn't have to be a step back. The fact that he was frightened he might start using again didn't automatically mean he was doomed to start using again.

Or maybe...

Swift dug through his desk until he found his old address book with the phone number for Barry Matuszak. Barry had been his sponsor at Cocaine Anonymous. Once he'd known the number by heart. Now he read it digit by digit from the small leather book and dialed.

The last time he'd talked to Barry had been eighteen months ago. Barry had called to say hi and see how he was doing. He'd been like that. Kind and conscientious. A good friend as well as a sponsor. There was a time when Swift had been unable to get through a day without talking to Barry, as helpless as a baby in his addiction recovery, but gradually he'd grown stronger, weaned himself, and eventually...grown away.

As fond as Swift was of Barry, as much as he liked and respected him, as grateful as he was to him, it had been necessary for him to break free in order to feel really well again. He had reached a point where he didn't want to be reminded that he was an addict, didn't want to think of himself as broken and ill.

"'Lo." The voice on the other end was raspy as though Swift had woken Barry. He glanced at the clock. Eight thirty. Barry couldn't be in bed already. Unless he was sick. There was a lot of flu going around.

"Barry? It's Swift."

There was a silence and then Barry cleared his throat. "Swift. How are you?"

"I'm...all right. How are you?"

"Good." Barry sounded brisker now, more like his old self. "It's been a while."

"I know. It's just..."

"Oh, I understand. Believe me. Still enjoying teaching?"

Barry taught too. Or had. He was retired now. He did

volunteer work at Long Creek Youth Development Center.

Swift talked for a while, basically filling in time till he had the nerve to say, "Barry, could we maybe get together and talk? Face to face?"

There was a pause before Barry said harshly, "You're using again."

"No," Swift refuted quickly. Just hearing the words had his stomach in knots. "I'm not. But I'm...it's on my mind. I can't seem to shake it."

"The craving is back." There was something dreadful and final in the way Barry said it. As though he were offering a terminal diagnosis, pronouncing sentence on Swift.

"It's stress. I know that's all it is, but the more I worry about it, the worse it is, and I thought if I could just talk to you for a while..."

"No."

For a second Swift wasn't sure he had heard correctly. "Barry, I'm not using. I promise. I'm not asking you to...I just need a little...help." The last word came out more shakily than he wanted.

"Call the Portland office. I've got the number right here." There was the slide of a desk drawer, a rattling of papers, and Barry began to recite a phone number.

"I don't want to call the Portland office. I just wanted to talk to y—"

"You can't be around me right now." Barry's voice was less harsh. "I can't help you. Call the office, Swift. Call Turk. Call him tonight."

"I'm not using." Swift wondered if he was going to break down. Why did no one believe him? Were they all so sure he was doomed to relapse? *Was* he doomed?

Barry spoke, his voice shaking. It took a few moments for the words to filter through. "*I'm* using again."

"What?"

"You heard me. I'm the last person you should be around right now. Call Turk. Call him now."

"How could—? What happened?"

Dial tone.

Eventually Swift remembered to put the handset down. He stared at the phone. Barry had been drug free for seventeen years. How was it even possible that he would relapse? And if Barry could fall, what the hell chance did Swift have?

He poured himself a glass of water and sat down at the table. His hands were shaking. Maybe if Swift had kept in touch...Barry didn't have anyone. No kids. He'd been married twice, but both his wives had left him before he'd gotten cleaned up.

You couldn't stay sober or drug free for someone else—that was an unfair burden to put on anyone—but having someone else to stay drug free and sober for did make a difference. It did for Swift.

He stared at the phone and then he dialed Max.

It was late. Murder investigation or no, Hannah was gone for the day and the automated answering system was on. Swift pressed Max's extension and prayed silently that Max was in the office.

Please. God. Please be there.

"Prescott." Max sounded preoccupied.

The relief left him weak. "Hi. It's me."

"Hi." Max's voice warmed, and Swift's tension eased another fraction.

"Are you going to be able to get over here tonight?"

"Tonight?" Max was regretful. "Tonight's not looking good."

Swift closed his eyes. You'd think that someone who had needed as much help as he had in his life would be good at asking for it. Not this time. He didn't want Max to think of him as anything but strong and whole and together.

But he wasn't. Not right now. And as much as he didn't want Max to think of him as weak, there was no one else he would trust with this terrible need. He took a deep breath. "I...even if it was late. I'd rather...not be on my own tonight."

Heat washed through him at the silence on the other end of the phone.

"Okay, I'll come by. I'll try to get away sooner, but it's liable to be late."

Max's voice was so calm, so ordinary, that Swift's precarious control wavered. He managed a gruff, "Thanks."

"Are you okay till I get there?"

"Yeah."

"See you then."

Swift was grateful that Max didn't press him for details, didn't make a bigger thing of it. That he simply hung up.

And knowing that Max was coming by steadied Swift. Just a few hours to get through and then he'd have company. He'd have Max. And even though Max would not be pleased with everything Swift had to tell him, he knew Max well enough to know Max would see him through the night.

One night at a time. That's how he'd done it the first time, and there had been no Max to rely on. There had been nothing and no one but his determination to never fail again. It had worked then. It would work now.

In the meantime he would keep busy.

Swift got out a clipboard and began to jot down the notes of

Tad's predicament in an effort to get matters straight in his own mind.

What did he know for sure? Not much.

He knew that Mario Corelli had been shot to death, and he knew his body had been left on a state beach.

There was a lot more he didn't know—and had no idea how to find out, even if he'd wanted to. He didn't know if the weapon had been found or who the weapon had belonged to, and he didn't know if Corelli had been killed at the beach or if he had been killed elsewhere and his body moved.

Looking at the list of question marks, Swift remembered why he hated reading murder mysteries. Only the police could know the answer to these questions. It was obvious from his own unsuccessful attempts at talking to people that it simply wasn't that easy to get information out of people unless you had the authority of the police behind you.

Facts were what you needed in this kind of situation.

Swift was someone who generally relied on his instincts. His intuition about people. It worked well in figuring out how to teach them, but it was unlikely to be effective in crime solving. At least he'd never heard Max talk about intuition. He did talk about hunches from time to time, but Max probably considered a hunch as something separate from intuition. Either way, you couldn't take a hunch to court.

Swift shook his head and made a list of possible suspects and their motives as he understood them.

Tad Corelli had a troubled relationship with his father and had threatened to kill him. He had been beaten up the day of Corelli's murder, and he had disappeared shortly after. And pretty much everyone, including his friends—no matter how much they denied it—thought he'd killed his old man.

In Swift's opinion parents were more likely to kill their

children than children kill their parents, but he didn't know that for a fact. What he did know for a fact was that no one had supplied a very compelling motive for why Tad would kill his father. Sure Corelli had knocked Tad around, but since he'd apparently been doing it for years, why should Tad suddenly kill him now? What had changed?

The mob. Maybe the mob was somehow involved in Corelli's murder, but would the mob try and make it look like anything other than a mob hit? Wasn't that kind of the point? When the mob killed people they generally wanted it known they were unhappy. So as to send a message.

Anyway, Swift wasn't about to get anywhere near that. So next suspect?

Cora Corelli clearly had bitter feelings for her ex-husband. She loved her son and would obviously want to protect him from his father, but that resurrected the problem of *why kill Corelli now*? Was it simply a matter of the straw that broke the camel's back?

Cora had tried to frame Swift with that cocaine—Swift didn't care what Max said, he was certain Cora had concealed the coke in his bathroom—and she wouldn't do that unless she was trying to protect Tad or herself, right?

Although it was kind of weird because Cora had seemed to believe Swift was trying to help Tad. And Swift *was* trying to help Tad.

So forget Cora for now. She seemed like too obvious of a suspect anyway. Surely if she *had* killed her ex, she wouldn't continue to go around bad-mouthing him and saying he'd got what he deserved?

But then Nerine Corelli was even more obvious of a suspect. The wife or husband was *always* the first to come under suspicion. And Nerine apparently knew how to shoot well enough to be president of her gun club. Although if she'd used one of her own guns, the police would know, right?

She had two motives that Swift could see. She'd been having an affair—well, according to some rumors—and she would inherit whatever estate her husband left. Plus Nerine was still living with Corelli, so if there was a time factor, an issue of *I can't take one minute more of this,* it would most likely apply to Nerine, right?

Max would have already checked all this stuff out, and if he'd cleared Nerine—and it seemed like he had—that was pretty much that. Max would have done things like check Nerine's gun registration and her alibi.

And he'd have done the same thing for Bill McNeill, the former mayor of Stone Coast.

Which was just as well because Swift was not about to try questioning Bill McNeill. For one thing, McNeill would have no idea where Tad was, and for another, bad things happened to Swift every time he spoke to anyone about Corelli's murder.

It was weird Tad was so sure Nerine was having an affair with McNeill, and Ariel was so sure she wasn't. Maybe Tad had got the idea from Cora. Cora would have precedent for thinking that.

The idea of having an affair was peculiar to Swift. His parents had been soul mates, the concept of infidelity had been something that had no meaning or relevance to them. Swift himself had no interest in anyone but Max. But he was worldly enough to know that for most people having an affair didn't automatically mean you didn't love your spouse. Besides, cynical though it was, not everyone married for life. It *did* seem like an odd thing to have an affair with your political rival. Both Nerine and Cora agreed on one point: McNeill and Mario Corelli had nearly come to blows over *something.*

But Nerine had accused Bill McNeill of her husband's murder, so it seemed unlikely they were lovers.

Come to think of it, on paper Bill McNeill looked pretty suspicious.

Swift frowned down at his notes. Unfortunately it wasn't as simple as a mathematical equation.

One thing that haunted him with this new disappearance of Tad's was the fear that Tad might have taken his own life.

No. He wasn't going to think about that. More likely Tad had spooked and was on the run again.

So. Final suspect? The waiter. Tony Lascola had been fired by Corelli. But apparently he had an alibi.

Swift absently chewed the end of his pen. He was glad it was Max's job to hunt down the truth and cage it. The fact was, he truly didn't care who had killed Mario Corelli. Corelli was dead and nothing could change that. All Swift cared about was Tad. If Tad had killed his father, that in itself would be the punishment. That would be all the punishment any one man could bear...

He woke to a stiff neck and the sound of Max's key in the lock. Swift tossed back the afghan, and the forgotten clipboard with all his notes clattered to the floor as he jumped from the sofa.

He met Max in the arched entryway.

"I didn't think you'd still be awake." Max held him hard for a long minute, the prolonged hug the only sign that maybe this wasn't a normal evening.

"I fell asleep on the couch." Swift drew back. "Do you want something to eat? I made those lambchops you like."

"I grabbed a burger earlier. I wouldn't mind a drink."

Max let him go, and Swift moved away and poured them each a drink from the frosted-glass cabinet.

"Cheers." They touched their glasses in a friendly chime.

He could see the question in Max's eyes, and he wasn't ready to face it. He'd always believed that part of the success of their relationship was that they never really asked anything of each other. He was about to ask something it might not be in Max's nature to give.

Instead, Swift swallowed a mouthful of scotch and said, "Remember when I said I thought Tad had a girlfriend?"

Max nodded, his gaze alert.

"Her name is Ariel Rhoem. She's majoring in biochemistry."

The scar on Max's forehead crinkled. "You found this out how?"

"From a poem Tad wrote. It was called 'Ariel' and there's only one Ariel enrolled at CBC." He could see Max prepare to point out that there might be a dozen other possible Ariels or that this might not be the same Ariel. "It turned out that she *is* seeing Tad. Or was."

"You've already talked to her?" It took effort for Max to control the instant leap of anger. Swift appreciated that effort.

"I know. I shouldn't have."

"How the hell many times are we going to go through this, Swift?"

Good question. "This is it. I promise. I thought it was worth having one last shot at getting Tad to give himself up."

"So this Ariel knows where the Corelli kid is?"

"She said no. She was lying, but..."

"This is *why*—" Max cut himself off. He said in a voice kept level by sheer discipline, "Swift, I'm doing my best to keep you clear of the fallout from this, but you seem determined to run back into that burning barn. I can't protect you from the consequences of your actions. Do you see that?"

"I don't need you to *protect* me."

"The hell you don't. You don't understand—" Max stopped.

Maybe he didn't. Swift went doggedly on. "The temptation is to keep my mouth shut about all this, but you need to find Tad and maybe there's something useful here. I don't know. If there is, I don't see it." Swift fished under the sofa for the clipboard and handed it to Max.

Max took it, glowering down at Swift's spidery handwriting. "What's this supposed to be?"

"I've written down everything I can think of, everything anyone said to me that might be useful."

Max tossed the clipboard aside. His head dropped against the back of the sofa. He stared up at the blackened beams of the ascending rafters and let out a long—very long—breath. Finally, he turned and stared at Swift. "Swift. This is what *I* do. You're supposed to teach kids to write and appreciate literature, remember? I don't tell you how to teach. *Why* are you involving yourself in my case?"

"Because I *am* involved whether I want to be or not. Tad involved me when he—"

"Goddamn it."

Swift shut up.

"I'm doing my best not to lose it with you." Max stopped. A muscle twitched in his jaw. He leaned forward, took a long swallow of his drink, sat back, cradling the glass between his big hands. "You're not making this easy for me. You're not making it easy for either of us."

"I know you're angry. I'm telling you this because I don't want there to be any lies between us. Never again. Now that I've told you everything, I'm out of it."

"That's what you said before." That twitch jumped again in Max's jaw. He took another long swallow and put his drink down on the table. "When you called and said you didn't want to be alone tonight, is this why? You wanted to get this off your chest?"

Swift shook his head. "No." His throat felt parched, his mouth bone dry. It hurt to swallow. "No. That's something different. But if you're too pissed off to stay, I understand."

Max's eyes were hard, his face tense. Swift could see the muscles of his thighs bunch as he moved to rise, but...instead Max relaxed back against the sofa cushions. He studied Swift. He rubbed his chin.

"One of the things I always liked about you, Swift, was you were low maintenance. You've been more trouble in the last week than in all the years I've known you."

Swift's laugh was humorless.

"Oh fuck," Max said wearily. "Let's go to bed."

Swift nodded. Rose.

Max rose too. He glanced dismissingly at the clipboard. "And for the record, Corelli was *not* killed by the mob."

Chapter Twelve

You are a famous archeologist. You...

Hell, you're anything but what you actually are, which is a crack-brained—

"Come here." Max's voice floated into the darkness between them.

Swift scooted across the flannel distance, and Max wrapped his arm around him, pulling him still closer. Swift shifted so that he could rest his head on Max's broad shoulder. It was a good shoulder for that. He could feel the hard, steady pound of Max's heart beneath his ear.

"My parents have been together over sixty years." The tone was level, the words neutral.

Swift nodded, listening. Max didn't talk about his family much. Neither did Swift. The difference was, Max apparently got on well with his folks. That's what he called them. *My folks.* It sounded friendly and informal and cozy. Swift bet they were nice people. Nice folks.

"One of their rules is you don't go to bed angry."

"That's a good rule."

Max nuzzled him and then bit his ear.

"Ow!" Swift drew back as far as Max's arms allowed. "What was that?"

"I've never lied to you. Don't lie to me anymore."

"I don't. I won't."

"Not by omission, not by implication or inference, not by anything."

"Okay." Swift rubbed his ear. "Got it. Loud and clear. Loud and *ear.*"

It was a pretty lame attempt at humor. Max let out a sound that might have been amusement or might have been skepticism, and pulled Swift back down. They lay quietly for a few minutes. Swift listened for the slowing, the deepening of Max's breathing.

He told himself that just having Max here tonight was enough. He was even relieved that he needn't tell Max the whole sordid truth, that he was as helpless and hopeless as any crackhead Max had ever busted.

He wriggled more comfortably against Max, closed his eyes, trying to think about nothing but the slow, soothing slide of Max's hand down his spine.

"Why don't you just tell me whatever it is that has you in knots?" Max sounded perfectly wide awake.

Swift blinked into the darkness, considering. Hadn't they had enough drama for one evening? He warned, "It doesn't fall under the Low Maintenance heading."

"Tell me anyway."

It was painful to have to admit it, and to Max of all people, but Swift forced himself to put it into words. "Something's going on with me, and I don't understand it. It's been years since I felt this way, and I don't know if it's all in my head or if it's something else."

"Sure," Max said in the tone of someone who has no idea of what the other person is talking about.

"I'm a cocaine addict. I'm recovering, but...I'm still an addict."

Max sounded puzzled. "I know." It was ground they had covered a long time ago.

"I'll bet. Had you read my file before I told you?"

"Yep. The second time you invited me for dinner."

Swift wasn't surprised. "And it didn't scare you off?"

"You're a very good cook." Max's arm tightened around Swift. "I'm here, aren't I?"

Yes. He was. Very much so.

"It's been—I've felt that my addiction is under control. As much as it can be, but lately—"

Yeah, definitely not an admission to make to someone looking for low maintenance in a lover. It was a mistake to spill all this, but tonight Swift needed a friend as much as he needed a lover, and if Max was not his friend, the other was doomed anyway.

"Go on."

"Lately the...cravings have started up again. And I'm afraid. Terrified..."

Max kissed his forehead. "Okay. That's kind of what I figured was going on."

That was a surprise. Swift raised his head, trying to see through the darkness. "Did you?"

"Mm. You've asked for help twice in all the time I've known you. Tonight and when you couldn't get the fountain in the backyard to work."

Swift smiled faintly, remembering. "The first time we met," he pointed out. "When my car was hit."

"That was official. You were reporting an accident. You

weren't asking me personally for help."

True. Very true. Not an easy thing for him at any time, and even after they started seeing each other, he wouldn't have wanted to impose on Max.

It was as though Max picked up his brainwaves. "You did the right thing calling tonight."

"I did?"

He must have sounded startled. Max gave a funny half laugh. "You don't think so?"

"I don't know." Swift confessed, "I'm so tired I can't think straight. This addiction is like trying to hang onto a-a pack of rottweilers, and all the time they're pulling and tugging and charging at their leashes, and I'm trying to drag them back. I'm worn out with it." How worn out hadn't even registered until this instant. And now that he had started talking, he couldn't seem to stop, lulled by Max's almost-absent caresses.

"I don't know if I need to go back into rehab or...or what. Just the thought of it makes me sick, but ever since you pulled that fucking bag out of the john, I can't stop thinking about it. Wanting it. I mean, I *don't* want it, but..."

"But you do," Max said calmly. His stoic acceptance of the unacceptable was a relief. Not least because Max so often saw the world in absolutes. Yes or no. Good or evil. Up or down.

"It's not even that clear. My brain *doesn't* want it, but my body is...it's...I've got all the familiar old symptoms. And it's not stopping. My head starts pounding, my heart starts racing, my gut is churning butterflies... God, I can almost *smell* it."

"Did you smell it when it was stashed in the bathroom?"

That brought Swift up short. He gave a shaky laugh. "No."

"Too bad. I was thinking we could use you after we retire Sparky."

"Who?"

"Our drug-detection dog."

Swift laughed, though it was halfhearted. "I'll probably be looking for work soon enough. It's just...I thought it was behind me. That part of it, at least. Now I'm remembering the statistics and the fact is, the relapse rate for cocaine addiction is between ninety-four to ninety-nine percent. A lot of experts say it's not possible to recover, the most you can hope for is to manage the relapses."

"Now you're letting the numbers scare you." Max wasn't joking around anymore. "You've been clean for six years?"

"Six. Yeah." He wasn't surprised Max had remembered the exact number. It would be a fact that Max had an interest in. Police Chiefs could not afford junkie boyfriends. Not even casual junkie boyfriends. "Sorry." Swift wiped his eyes impatiently. "I know I'm dumping this on you and it's not like I expect you to have an answer. I just needed to tell someone."

"Six years drug free is huge. Remember that."

"It's not like seventeen years, though." He filled Max in on his failed attempt to get hold of his therapist and then the awful phone call to Barry. "If anybody could make it, I'd've bet anything it would have been Barry."

"I'm sorry about Barry. But you're not him. His failure doesn't mean your failure, any more than his success guaranteed yours." Max's caresses were more deliberate now, his hand a warm weight as he made soothing little circles in the small of Swift's back. "You're the captain of your own destiny."

Swift smiled tiredly. Did Max know the source of that quote? "I know."

"Just close your eyes and relax."

Gratefully, Swift closed his eyes, trying to concentrate on

nothing more than the feel of Max's hand rubbing his back. Such a simple, uncomplicated pleasure, that of touch. Max smoothed the thin skin between Swift's shoulder blades.

"This is where your wings used to be."

Swift expelled a half laugh, most of his attention fixed on the slow deliberate slide of Max's hand down his spine. Max's fingers brushed the final links of bone and cartilage. "And that's where my tail used to be," Swift murmured.

Max made an amused sound. He traced a light finger down Swift's crack. Swift shivered in instant response. Despite his exhaustion, he was still too wound up to sleep, so if this was turning sexual, it was fine by him. He welcomed the distraction.

Max palmed his ass cheek beneath the blankets, stroking and petting, every so often his fingertip brushing the opening to Swift's body. It felt nice, very nice. Swift waited, aroused and anticipating whatever Max had in mind.

Without warning, Max pushed his finger inside. Swift jerked, the sound he made high and startled to his own ears.

"Shhh. Stay with me." Like there was a chance Swift was going somewhere? Max moved his finger knowingly in that tight, hot channel. Without the lube it scraped, even hurt a little, but Max nuzzled his shoulder, and he was touching Swift so sweetly, so pleasingly. "You like that?"

Swift nodded. He didn't like pain, but this odd mix of sensation wasn't exactly pain. He wasn't sure what it was, but it required his full consideration.

Max whispered, "Move onto your side."

Swift rolled onto his side, and Max spooned closer, his other hand wrapping around Swift's cock. Swift murmured approval, instinctively pushing up into Max's firm grasp while aware that Max had slid the finger in Swift's ass deeper still—all the way to his knuckle—and then out so that Swift could feel the tiny bite of fingernail on his anus.

Swift caught his breath. It was almost dizzyingly intimate, that careful, possessive in and out. In and out. Again. And again. A small burn to accompany the press of pleasure. He shivered again as Max tongued the back of his neck. So much loving attention from every direction. It was bewildering and reassuring. Max was working his cock with one hand and finger fucking him with the other. No effort was required from Swift at all, and he could feel all his tension and conflict unraveling beneath that expert touch.

They'd tried a number of things through the years, taking turns with everything. He'd certainly had Max's fingers up his ass, but in the past it had been a means to an end. Tonight, this was apparently the end, this alarmingly tender onslaught.

Nice to be catered to. His body could take this with no strain at all. He didn't even have to thi—

Max slid another dry, blunt finger into Swift.

Swift gasped, squirmed, but accepted it. Usually he preferred a light touch, but tonight this more aggressive approach was just right. He *couldn't* think about anything else, the delicious assaults on his body ensured that. The lack of warning, of preparation, turned out to be what he needed.

His heart was thundering, his breath coming in winded pants as every few seconds Max changed things up again. A hot tongue in his ear, a little nip on the curve of his throat, and that combination of finger massaging his prostate and hand stroking his cock was creating a sort of sensory overload—satisfaction so intense it was dizzying. It was almost pain—and yet far too sweet for pain.

And it didn't stop. It went on and on until he began to wonder if his much misused body could stand the strain. From a long way away he could hear the noises he was making, wild little sounds from the back of his throat as he gave into it everything Max was doing to him.

Max whispered to him, saying lovely, foolish things, heated words against Swift's ear, telling Swift how beautiful he was, how much Max liked the way he moved, the sounds he made, and the delectable things that Max was going to do to him.

When orgasm at last tore through Swift it was something closer to violence than pleasure, but it brought a purging relief in its hot, wet wake. Or maybe he was just too numb after all that to feel anything at all. Too tired to move, for sure.

Max gathered him closer still, winding him tightly in his arms. "Are you listening, Swift?"

Swift nodded in exhausted assent.

"Sleep. You're worn out. It's okay to let go. I've got you."

Swift's throat closed. Maybe Max understood that he couldn't speak, even if he'd known what to say.

"I'm not going to let go of you. I'm going to hold you all night. So go ahead and feel whatever you feel. If you're still craving cocaine, go ahead. You're safe. You can crave it all you want, but I won't let go, and if you still feel like you can't trust yourself in the morning, and it's what you want, I'll drive you to rehab myself. Okay?"

Stupid, so stupid that it should get to him like that. But it did. Hot tears spilled over and itched their way down his face. He wiped them on his shoulder. "Thanks."

He felt Max shake his head. "There's not much I won't do for you, Swift. You ought to know by now."

He slept like the dead. If he dreamed, he wasn't aware of it. He woke with Max's arms wrapped around his torso and Max's genitals soft against his ass. And for the first time in days he wasn't aware of wanting anything but breakfast. Breakfast and Max. Not necessarily in that order.

Max was tired, though. Swift could see the lines of fatigue that hadn't quite smoothed out during the night. There were threads of silver in Max's brown hair and even in his mustache, and the recognition of Max's mortality squeezed Swift's heart.

He lay still, even regulating his breathing, savoring the peace of being together like this, doing nothing that might wake Max too soon.

Three minutes before the alarm went off, Max's eyelashes flickered and rose. He gazed wordlessly at Swift. Swift smiled ruefully. Max lifted a hand and stroked his knuckles down Swift's prickly cheek. His mouth curved in faint response. No words needed.

They showered and dressed in that same peaceful wordless understanding, and over the usual toast and coffee spoke of nothing more serious than the drizzle fogging up the kitchen windows.

Before Max left he said, "If things get on top of you today, call me." His eyebrows rose in response to whatever he read in Swift's face. "Now what?"

"I just...didn't expect this."

"What did you expect?"

With one—maybe one and a half—notable exceptions, they had always been honest with each other. "I thought you might see me through whatever last night was and then suggest we take a break for a while. Put a safe distance between us."

Max grunted. "Did you see any other possibilities?"

"I didn't let myself look for them."

Max said nothing.

"Why *are* you doing this? You said it yourself last night. If anything I've—our friendship has been a bigger hassle in the last six days than in all the last six years."

"That's sure as hell true." Max's grin was wry. "I guess...maybe I like to be needed."

If that were true, he'd have to travel a distance to find anyone needier than Swift. It was a bitter thought.

"Or maybe..."

"Maybe what?"

Max's smile faded. He actually seemed to lose some of his normal healthy color as he said, "Maybe it turns out that I love you."

Love. Swift's heart seemed to stumble. Not "have feelings" or "care for you". No. The L-word. Not just naked. The full monty. "Do you?"

"Yeah. I think I do."

"You...think?"

Max said seriously, "I've thought so since the night I kicked you out of my office. Anyone else, I'd have slapped with more charges than a box of Eveready batteries."

"Now that you mention it, I was surprised you let me walk out of there. Grateful. But surprised."

"So was I. I was more surprised when I realized I was as worried about what you'd done to your career as what you'd done to my homicide investigation. I couldn't figure out what to do. I had to stay away from you."

Swift nodded. The staying away had hurt.

"When I interviewed you in your classroom, I was still angry."

"I know."

"But I knew..."

Swift's smile was twisted. "I'll be the first to admit my judgment is probably impaired. Cocaine addiction being a possible symptom rather than cause."

"You were motivated by kindness and the desire to help. I don't get a lot of that in my line of work. So I'll take the impaired judgment and good heart over...anything else I've seen." He added as Swift opened his mouth, "It doesn't hurt that it all comes in a very pretty package."

"I don't think you should mention my package if either of us are planning to go into work."

Max laughed and kissed Swift. "True. Stay out of trouble."

"It'll be my pleasure, Chief."

Swift stuck to that all day. No calling people and asking questions they didn't want to answer, no chasing after people who didn't want to be found. He'd tried to help but he'd failed. You could only do what you could do.

The call came through just as he was leaving for the afternoon.

"This caller refuses to identify himself." Dottie's voice crackled with irritation. One more thing Swift was deliberately doing to annoy her was the implication.

"Thanks. I'll take it."

She transferred the call without further word.

"Swift."

The response was blurred. He couldn't make out the words. Swift's scalp prickled. "I'm sorry?"

"I'm at the cottage. On Orson Island," the muffled voice said more distinctly. "Can you come? Can you come right away?"

"Tad?"

"Yes. Will you come, Professor? Alone."

"What's going on? You've got to come in and give yourself up." Swift leaned forward, pressing the earpiece closer, trying to make out the thick syllables.

"Please. I will. But I have to talk to you first, Professor. Just you. No one else."

Swift thought rapidly. "All right. But it'll take me a while to get out to the island. Are you okay till I get there?"

"Yes. Yes, but please hurry."

The phone went dead. Swift replaced the handset, then picked it up again and dialed Max.

It took a few minutes to get through. "Hey, can I call you back?" Max greeted him brusquely.

"Max, I just got a call from someone claiming to be Tad."

"Claiming? You don't think it's Tad?"

"I don't know. I doubt it. To me it sounded like someone talking through a handkerchief. Not that I'm an expert."

"What did the caller want?"

"He—I think it was a he—wants me to go out to Orson Island. He said he had something to tell me and that I had to come alone."

"You are fucking kidding me."

"I know. Even *I* know enough to recognize it's a trap. But I don't get the point of it."

"The point is someone's trying to set you up."

"Me or Tad? Or both?"

"Go home. I'll take it from here."

"Wait." Swift didn't give Max a chance to override him. "I think I should go."

"*What?* No. Way. No fucking way. *Go home.*"

"*Wait.* Listen. You want to catch this guy, right? Whoever he is? You'll scare him off if you show up with cop cars and flashing lights."

"Good idea. We won't flash our lights."

Swift ignored Max's sarcasm. "I'm serious. Use me for bait."

"Remember that thing about impaired judgment? Here's an example."

Nice to know they hadn't lost the ability to be frank. Swift shot back, "Fuck you, Max. If you'd look at this objectively, you'd know I'm right. If it's a trap, then this guy is going to be watching to see that I show up and nobody else. And if it's not a trap—"

"No."

"All I'm suggesting is that I go to the island with you, that we take my car, and that I let you out before I get to the bungalow. That way you can grab him before he can make a move."

"I said no."

"Why? For God's sake *why*? It's the perfect chance to turn this trap on whoever set it up because whoever set it up *also* obviously thinks my judgment is impaired and that I'm going to walk right into this. Whatever it is."

"Go figure."

"Is it concern for me making you such an asshole, because otherwise I don't get your attitude."

There was a sharp silence.

"Truth?" Max said tersely. "I'm afraid you're going to ignore what I'm telling you and go out to the island anyway."

The honesty disarmed Swift. "Give me a little credit. If you won't agree to my plan, I'll leave it there. But at least consider what I'm saying. If Tad didn't call me, then whoever this is...it's someone you want to question, right? If you go on your own, he'll see you coming a mile away. If you come with me, you'll have a better shot of grabbing him."

"What the hell makes you think he won't shoot you the minute you step out of your car?"

"I don't know. I don't know why the plan would be to kill *me,* though. Wouldn't it be more likely...?"

"Yes?" Max inquired dryly.

"I don't know. But why would anyone want me dead? It's more logical that he's planting some evidence at the bungalow that I'm meant to find, don't you think? Something that will incriminate Tad beyond reasonable doubt."

"Or it may be Tad himself."

"Or it may be, yeah."

Swift could practically hear Max's thoughts. At last Max growled, "I don't like it."

At that irritable rumble, Swift relaxed, knowing the battle was won. "Me neither. But so what?"

"If we do this, you don't get out of the car. Understand? You drive up to the bungalow and you stay inside the car."

"Okay."

Max swore. He said crisply, "I'll meet you at the ferry in twenty minutes."

"See you there." Swift hung up. Having succeeded in convincing Max to his way of thinking, he was surprised he didn't feel happier.

Chapter Thirteen

You have traveled back in time to one of the first Olympic Games held in ancient Greece. The competition is about to begin and you are one of the challengers. Will you choose to compete in the pankration or the pentathlon?

Or, considering that you're a poet and not an athlete, maybe you oughta just stay home and write a nice ode to something.

"Remember, you don't get out of the car," Max said.

The car tires crunched on gravel as they wound their way up the dirt road to the bungalow. The sound of the engine drifted in the clear, cold air.

Swift replied, "The last thing I plan on doing is getting out of this car."

One of the three deputies in the backseat of Swift's Jeep snickered. The entire police force of Stone Coast, minus Hannah Maltz, was on the way to Swift's bungalow—and whoever was waiting for them.

"Don't forget to slow down from the point you let us out. Give us time to get into position."

"Right." This was the third time Max had reminded him of this, which indicated how uneasy with the setup Max was. That made two of them.

"And if anything strikes you as off—I mean *anything*—get the hell out of there."

Swift nodded. He reminded himself it had been his bright idea to tag along.

He took his foot off the gas as he spotted the place a few yards ahead where he planned to let Max and his deputies out. The road dipped down and the trees sheltered it from the bungalow, but it was still close enough that it should only take Max and his men a couple of minutes to race up the hillside.

Swift slowed, pulled to the side and rolled to a stop. Max pushed open the Jeep passenger-side door, and he and his deputies scrambled out into the autumn woods.

Max's eyes met Swift's. He didn't say anything. Neither did Swift. Max eased the door shut.

Swift continued slowly up the road, part of his mind registering the diffused autumn twilight glancing off the red and gold leaves, unconsciously testing the words to describe such beauty—part of his mind worrying over what might be waiting ahead.

The bungalow swung into view. It looked unchanged from the last time Swift had been there. No smoke from the chimney, no lights shining behind the curtains.

He parked in the front yard, leaving the engine still running, watching and waiting for the front door to open.

The door did not open. Nothing moved behind the windows.

Swift studied the trees and rocks surrounding the clearing and the bungalow. No sign of life. Were Max and his people in position yet? How would he know?

What if no one was here? What if the phone call had been a prank? A practical joke? On the whole Swift decided he would prefer that embarrassment to the horror of finding something awful inside the bungalow. Some bloodstained clue or the murder weapon or something even worse. A body. Tad's body.

That was the fear that wouldn't be banished. That Tad was dead. And, most terrifyingly, by his hand.

Swift shuddered. Why had he thought this was such a great idea? Such a great idea that he had argued Max, who knew better, into it?

He checked the rearview mirror. Drummed his fingers on the steering wheel. It was going to look weird if he didn't get out of the Jeep, but he'd told Max he would stay in his vehicle and that's what he intended to do. Instead, he gave two short blasts of the horn.

Not normal behavior at all. Bound to alert whoever was inside the cabin that something was up.

He caught a flash of red out of the corner of his eye. Swift turned his head in time to see a cardinal fly from a branch and disappear into the flame-colored foliage. He relaxed.

The windshield shattered. Something thumped the edge of the passenger seat, and stuffing floated up like tiny yellow clouds. A few glittering pieces of glass scattered over Swift's hands where they gripped the steering wheel.

If he hadn't already been nervous and on edge, it might have been a different story, but because he'd been waiting for something to happen, there was only a split second of disbelief that it actually *had*, and then he was sliding down, crouching as far as he could get—which, given the cramped quarters of the Jeep, wasn't far—as another bullet punched his seat. Squarely in the center of the seat. Perfect for blasting a hole through his heart and spine. He heard the ping of something metallic as the bullet passed on through the Jeep interior, and he could hear the terrified thunder of his heart, and then more shots.

Jesus fucking *Christ.*

He could hear Max yelling, but he couldn't make out the words over the hissing of the Jeep engine.

Max had told him to get the hell out of there if something happened, but Swift hadn't considered this possibility, and he didn't dare sit up. With his foot off the brake, the Jeep was starting to gently roll backwards, and while *away* seemed like a great idea, Swift remembered that if the Jeep went off the road and started down the hillside, he was liable to end up on the beach below.

He felt around frantically for the gearbox, tried to stomp his foot on the brake and then tried to use his hand. He was relatively limber thanks to all the yoga he did, but there was no room for maneuvering. It was like being in a very small cage or a metal straitjacket.

He reached for the steering wheel and hauled it the opposite way. He wasn't trying to steer, since he couldn't see which way he was going, so much as slow the vehicle's progression.

The passenger-side door yanked open, and he put his arms up protectively.

"It's me." Max jumped half inside, crowding his leg over the gearbox so he could jam on the brakes. He yanked the parking brake, and the Jeep rocked to a stop. "Are you hit?"

"No."

"Stay down."

He was gone.

Swift angled to try and see from the passenger-side mirror, and he caught a glimpse of Max loping down the road, his pistol held low and ready in both hands.

Swift dropped back and stared up through the crackled

window at the clouds tumbling like gray glaciers through the blue-water. Crimson leaves were stark against the dusk. It reminded him of something. He couldn't think what.

It seemed only a minute or two, counted out by the gonging of Swift's heart, before he heard the bite of boots on the road and the Jeep door flew open once more.

Swift jumped and then relaxed—though relaxed was probably not the right word for the current arrangement of his limbs.

"What yoga position is that?" Max inquired in a perfectly ordinary voice.

"Folding hero." Swift took the hand Max extended and uncoiled painfully from his cramped position beneath the dashboard.

"Looks like hero showing good sense to me."

"Is everyone okay?"

"Yep. Norman whacked his forehead on a branch. Maybe it'll knock some sense into him."

"Did the bad guy get away?"

"He won't get far unless he's one hell of a swimmer. I've got two deputies posted at the ferry. Did you get a look at the shooter?"

Swift shook his head.

"Neither did we. Just a camo jacket and a hunting cap." He studied Swift critically. "Close your eyes." He brushed the broken glass out of Swift's hair, then dusted it lightly, carefully, from his cheeks. Swift felt the tiny burn across his cheekbones.

"You were right. This was not a good idea."

Max grunted. "It wasn't the idea itself that was bad. It was your participation I had a problem with."

165

Swift opened his eyes. "Your fingers are shaking."

Max nodded. "Adrenaline. It's pretty exciting seeing your friend's car get shot full of holes. Especially with your friend sitting inside."

Swift nodded too. "From my side too." He spotted one of Max's deputies circling around the bungalow. "I want to check inside the house. Make sure nothing—no one is..."

He didn't have to finish it. Max nodded. His expression was as grim as Swift's thoughts.

But when they tried the door, it was locked. Swift used his key, they stepped inside.

It took a second for his eyes to adjust to the gloom. Swift scanned the room. To his abject gratitude there was no body sprawled on the rug in front of the fireplace.

"No one's been inside since I was here a week ago." He didn't bother to disguise his relief.

"Doesn't look like it." Max looked around curiously at the stone fireplace, the open beams, the comfortable, faded furniture. The deputy investigating the perimeter of the bungalow passed briefly by the window. "So this is where you come when you want to get away?"

"This is it."

"It's quiet."

Neither spoke, and the waves from the beach below filled the silence.

"Am I one of the things you want to get away from?"

Swift stared at Max, not comprehending for a second. "Let me show you something." He led the way to the bedroom and picked up the copy of *Who Killed Harlowe Thrombey?* from where he'd left it lying his last visit. He removed the postcard bookmark with its quote from *The Tempest*. "Remember this?"

Max was smiling at the book. "I remember these. I used to have a stack of them." He took the bookmark. His smile grew odd. "Oh yeah. This. I thought when you came back early that things would change."

"I thought they would too."

The deputy banged on the front door and they both jumped.

"Timing is everything," Max said, and Swift wasn't sure if he meant the postcard or the interruption, but either way the moment was gone.

By the time they finished on the island and made it back to the mainland it was after seven. The Portland police as well as the Coast Guard had joined in the search for the escaped shooter, but the man had vanished completely.

Swift's wounded Jeep was towed back to the ferry and then to a garage in Portland. Max drove him home.

"I can't stay. I've got a pile of paperwork to fill out." Max followed him inside. "Reporters to deal with. A city council to calm down."

And a murder yet to solve.

Swift's phone began to shrill as they passed through the entryway, the sound spiking off the beams and hardwood floors, and making them both jump.

Swift swore.

"Christ. Let it ring," Max advised. His voice was raspy from giving orders all evening.

"Like you would?" Swift picked up the phone as Max went to pour himself a drink.

"I've been trying and trying to get a hold of you," a voice

167

cried on the other end of the phone.

Swift's stomach dropped a flight or two. "*What?*"

"It wasn't me." The voice was now recognizably Tad's though he sounded distraught and exhausted. His voice dragged with fatigue. "I heard on the news. It wasn't me, Professor Swift. I promise. I have no reason to want to hurt you. I wasn't anywhere near Orson Island."

"Where are you, Tad?"

Max's head turned sharply his way.

The only sound on the other end of the line was heavy breathing that seemed close to tears.

"Enough is enough," Swift said. "Where the hell are you? I'm coming to get you, and you're going to give yourself up to the police. Do you understand?"

Max was beside him. He mouthed, "Get him to hang on the line."

"I'm so tired. I feel like I haven't stopped running since...since it happened. But if I give myself up, they'll stop looking for whoever killed my..." Tad's voice cracked.

Max was on his cell phone requesting a phone trace. Swift said into the phone, "That's bullshit, Tad. And someone is using that bullshit fear of yours against you. If something had happened to me today, you'd be the number-one suspect. Do you not see that?"

"I heard the news. The police think it was me. It wasn't me!"

"Where are you?"

Tad continued to breathe heavily into the phone.

"Where. Are. You?" Swift snapped.

"The Seabird Motel on the outskirts of town."

"What room?"

"One oh nine."

"Stay put. I'm coming to get you." Swift put down the phone.

"Anything?" Max asked into his cell. To Swift, he said, "Where is he?"

"Will you let me bring him in?"

"Never mind," Max said into his phone. He disconnected. To Swift, he said, "No. Where is he?"

"Max—"

"No." Max was already shrugging back into his coat. "A— your car's in the shop. B—we tried it your way today and you nearly got your head blown off. Or have you forgotten already?"

"I haven't forgotten. But we knew that was a trap. This *is* Tad."

"We don't know that this afternoon wasn't Tad too."

"He's got no reason to want to kill me."

"We don't know that. What we do know is *someone* thinks they've got a good reason to kill you."

"I don't believe this is personal."

"What kind of comment is that?"

That was the question, wasn't it? Swift wasn't sure what kind of comment it was. If someone had shot at him out of the blue, Swift would have figured the list of suspects might reasonably include everyone he'd ever flunked to his English Department archenemy Dottie. One was no more ludicrous than the other.

But it was too big a coincidence that at the same time Tad was in such desperate trouble, someone's dislike of Swift soared to homicidal on the crazy thermostat. Of course there was a connection.

"I think if someone wants me dead, it's only because it'll help build the case against Tad."

Max wasn't listening anyway. He cracked open his pistol and checked the cylinder. He holstered it.

"Jesus. You don't need a gun. He's not dangerous." Swift stepped in front of Max. "At least let me go with you. He's liable to panic if he sees you show up with a bunch of deputies."

"Butt out, Swift." It wasn't unkind, but it *was* adamant. "This time we're doing it my way. I'll do my best to bring the kid in without hurting a hair on his head, okay? But that's partly up to him. Now where is he?"

When Swift hesitated, Max said, "*Swift,* I made bad choices on that island this afternoon because I was worried about your safety. I can't do my job if my mind's on you. Do you understand?"

Swift understood. He wasn't sure if he was shocked or flattered or both. What mistakes had Max made?

"The Seabird Motel. Room one oh nine. Max, he's scared to death. He's liable to panic."

Max grabbed Swift's shoulder in a hard, fleeting squeeze. "I know. I've done this before. Trust me. Okay? Like I've been trusting you."

Swift was still blinking over that when the door closed behind Max.

He spent a tense seventy minutes pacing up and down the length of the old church before the phone rang again.

He snatched the phone up on the first ring.

"The Corelli kid's fine," Max said before Swift got the breath to speak. "Not so much as a split lip on either side. We've got him booked, and he's all snuggled up in his cell for the night."

"Can I see him?"

The sigh was audible. "He's not asking for you, but...I guess. Tomorrow."

Swift sagged against the wall. "Did he say anything?"

"Besides *I didn't do it*? No. He's waiting for his lawyer."

"Do you believe him?"

"I'd be more likely to believe him if he'd say what did happen that afternoon. Demanding a lawyer isn't exactly a mark of innocence."

"But you can't blame him at this point."

"I didn't say I blamed him, but I've yet to hear anything that justifies your faith in him."

"It's his father's funeral tomorrow."

"I know that."

"Are you going to let him attend?"

"I guess I'll figure something out."

Swift cleared his throat. "Are you coming by tonight?"

"Between the snafu on the island and arresting your protégé, that mountain of paperwork just keeps getting higher. If you're okay, I need to stay here and catch up."

"I'm fine." Swift realized he'd managed to get through the entire day without more than the occasional twinge of need. Things were back to normal. Nothing like nearly getting your head blown off to focus your priorities. "I'll miss you, though."

There was an underlying smile in Max's "Yeah? Well, it's mutual, Teach."

Swift hung up and went into the kitchen. He fixed himself tea and sat down at the table, absently studying the recently mopped and gleaming floor.

Nerine owned a rifle. She probably owned a couple of rifles.

171

She said she believed in Tad's innocence, and yet a huge part of the case against Tad came from Nerine's casual remarks. And if she hadn't lied, she certainly had some gaps in her knowledge of her stepson. She'd indicated Tad had a serious drug problem, but it turned out to be no more than a couple of joints. She'd said Hodge Williams was Tad's only close friend, but everyone else Swift talked to always mentioned Denny Jensen and Hodge in the same breath.

Why? Why the exaggerations and misdirection?

Here and there where the lamplight touched the blue-green granite it seemed to glint like starlight off the sea, like the short, sparkling stretch of ocean between the mainland and Orson Island.

He stared at those pinpoints of light, so bright they seemed to dazzle his eyes.

Slowly he rose and walked to the phone.

"It's me," he said when Max answered at last.

"What's up?"

"My housekeeper. Can you find out who she was before she was Mrs. Ord?"

Chapter Fourteen

You are hiking through Serpent Valley when you stumble upon the mysterious Caverns of Eternity. As you journey farther into the great cavern you discover it branches off into two passageways. One curves downward to the left; the other leads upward to the right. Is it possible that the one leading down is a channel to the past and the one leading up is a path to future? Which way will you choose?

In the old days Swift had always chosen the future. Now...he'd have taken the past—and the opportunity to change things—in a second.

But that's not the way life worked. There were no do-overs. If you screwed up, there was no magical way to go back and put it right. You had to fix it the best you could—and sometimes there was no fixing it.

He was thinking of that as he listened to Tad's halting explanation in the police station the next morning.

"My dad and I fought, yeah, and I said some things I regret and I know he did things he regretted too. He had a temper. Italian, you know? But I know he loved me. And I *loved* him. He was my dad. I didn't kill him, Professor Swift."

"What did you fight about?"

"When?"

"Before this happened."

"We-we didn't."

One of the deputies looked into the cell and glanced meaningfully at his watch. Tad's mouth tightened. Swift nodded acknowledgment and the deputy withdrew.

"What did you usually fight about?"

"I don't know. He wasn't happy when I quit football. That was the big thing. I lost my scholarship when I quit playing, so it was expensive. For my dad. My schooling and having to pay back the scholarship and all that. He kind of had a point, I guess."

"You couldn't play football and still—"

"No."

That was pretty definite. "If you didn't fight with your dad, how did you get battered?"

The worst of the bruising had faded, but there were still shadow splotches of yellow and purple on Tad's drawn face. He'd lost weight during his days on the run.

Tad stared down at his hands. "I got into it with some of the guys from the football team."

"Got into it over what?"

Tad's eyes rose briefly to Swift's and then fell again. "They were pissed about my quitting the team."

"What? But you quit the team over a year ago."

Nothing from Tad.

"That's kind of a delayed reaction."

Nothing.

"You're saying your old teammates beat you up because you don't want to play football anymore?"

Tad shrugged, staring down at his clasped hands.

"That doesn't make sense."

Tad's jaw took on a mulish jut, but he still didn't speak.

"Were Hodge and Denny part of that?"

"No."

They seemed to be getting nowhere fast. Swift wracked his brain. He remembered Cora's comments about Hodge and Tad being former best friends. He remembered Hodge saying Tad's troubles were all Swift's fault.

Swift said slowly, "But this all has something to do with being in the Lighthouse program?"

Tad's hands clenched and unclenched. Big hands. A man's hands. But Tad was a boy. His fingernails were bitten down to the quick. Swift stared at the ragged nails. He considered the way Tad kept avoiding his eyes.

Swift remembered Dr. Koltz's strange comments.

Slowly it began to dawn on Swift what was making Tad so awkward. "Did they—these guys from the football team—do they think you're gay?"

He could tell by the color flooding Tad's face that he'd nailed it. Tad went scarlet and then white. He nodded.

"They bashed you for being gay, but...you're not gay."

Tad finally looked up. "Try telling those dickheads that. They think anyone who wants to write poetry has to be a—" He flushed red again.

"Faggot?"

Tad's lips pressed so tight they looked bloodless.

Swift assimilated this. "Why didn't you report it? Why didn't you just come out and tell me what had happened when you came to my office? I could have done something."

Tad burst out, "That would have made it worse!"

"How?"

Tad was looking at Swift as though Swift just didn't get it—and that was perfectly correct because Swift *didn't* get it.

Drawing a rough breath, Tad said, "Professor Swift, you don't care what people say about you. If I went public with what happened to me, it would just spread the rumor wider. It wouldn't matter what I said. People are gonna believe what they want."

Well, that explained a few things.

Swift said, "You're right. I don't care what people say about me, if what they're saying is I'm gay. That's the truth. If they say something that's not true, I do care about that. I mean, depending on what the thing is. There are some things too stupid to bother with. But there are other things that have to be addressed. If this bothers you—and it does—you have to address it."

"It doesn't bother me," Tad snapped. "It's none of their fucking business. You've been...great to me. I'm not going to..."

"You're not going to what?"

Tad shook his head miserably.

Swift put a hand to his forehead. "Wait a minute. Do you somehow think you're being disloyal to me if you defend yourself?"

"No. I don't know. They're always talking about getting rid of you. Firing you, I mean."

That pulled Swift up short like nothing else could have. "Who is?"

"Some of the parents and some of the kids." Tad clarified, in case Swift was still missing the point, "Because you're gay."

"Are you serious?"

Tad nodded.

It turned out Max wasn't wrong about Swift living in his own world, because he'd never had a clue. Oh, he knew he wasn't in the running for Teacher of the Year, but it hadn't dawned on him how unpopular he might be in some quarters.

His position was vulnerable. He didn't have tenure. The title of professor was honorary and courtesy. He had been hired by Koltz's predecessor because he was the scion of a literary dynasty and sort of a celebrity in his own right, even if most people who knew of him knew of him for all the wrong reasons. He was a conscientious and competent instructor and he'd done a nice job with the *Pentagoet Review*, but he knew perfectly well that he'd really got the job based on the assumption that he'd eventually start writing again and that when that happened he'd be batting, as it were, for the home team.

After all, poets wrote...poetry. It wasn't an unrealistic expectation. In fact, for a long time it had been Swift's own expectation.

"And that's why you didn't want to tell me you'd been gay bashed. Mistakenly gay bashed, that is?"

Tad nodded.

"And you wanted time to think because you're trying to decide if you should, what? Transfer out?"

Another nod.

Swift could see the appeal of trying to start over some place completely new. That had been his own tactic when faced with rebuilding his life. But his own situation had been a lot more dire—nor had there been anything left to hold him to his old life.

That wasn't the case for Tad.

He said more gently, "Doesn't that seem a little drastic?"

"I don't know. Then I heard about my...and everyone was

177

thinking *I'd* done it, that *I'd* killed my dad." He stared at Swift in horror. "That they could *think* that..."

Swift understood that pain only too well. "The main reason they think it is because you went on the run."

"I went on the run because they thought I did it."

"God." Swift sighed. "Why the hell didn't you go to the bungalow?"

Color flooded Tad's face again. "That would just make it worse if anyone found out."

Oh. Right. Professor Swift's love shack. "Where did you go?"

"Ariel's grandparents have a place at Wolfe Neck. I camped out there."

"And what was your plan?"

"Plan?"

That was a kid for you. Tad looked so blank Swift nearly laughed. "You must have had some plan, right? You weren't thinking you could live the rest of your life skulking on the outskirts of town."

"Oh. I thought—we *all* thought—"

"Who's *we*?"

"Ariel, Hodge, Denny and me. We all thought if I could avoid getting arrested long enough, maybe Chief Prescott would catch the guy who killed my dad."

Oh yeah. That.

Swift watched Tad closely. "Do you know who killed your dad?"

Tad was watching Swift too. "No."

"But you have a theory?"

"No."

"No theory at all?"

Tad said reluctantly, "I don't know. Maybe Bill McNeill."

"That's what your stepmother says too."

Tad didn't say anything.

"Why do you think Bill McNeill would kill your father?"

"I don't." He wiped his face. "I don't know. They used to get into it sometimes, Dad and McNeill."

"Over what?"

"Business. And..."

"And?"

Tad shook his head.

Swift said neutrally, "Your mother thinks your stepmother might be guilty."

There was no mistaking the emotion that twisted Tad's features. "I *know* Nerine did it," he said bitterly. "Even if she didn't pull the trigger. But you'll never get anyone to believe that. You'll never prove it."

There was something convincing about that hopeless conviction. Tad might be wrong, but there was no doubt he believed what he was saying.

"Why would your stepmother want your father out of the way?"

Tad wiped at the tears welling in the corners of his eyes. "Because she's a selfish, conniving *bitch*. She deliberately took my dad away from my mom. She pretended to be having a baby, but then there was no baby. She said she *lost* it. Where? Macy's? I'm surprised she'd notice."

"Is there anyone else Nerine—"

"Nerine uses people." Tad's mouth trembled. "She manipulates them. People just see that she's pretty and she's smart. They don't see how cold she is underneath it. If McNeill

179

killed my dad, she's behind it. She's the *only* person with anything to gain."

"That's hard to say. Someone might think they had something to gain even though it isn't anything the rest of us can see."

"Like what?" Tad's forehead wrinkled as it did when Swift was introducing new and complicated concepts in class.

Swift wasn't sure himself. "Did Nerine and your dad fight a lot?"

"Not like my dad and mom. Mostly it was Dad accusing her of flirting around and Nerine accusing my dad of being jealous."

"Of Bill McNeill."

"Mostly. Yeah."

"And you told all that to Chief Prescott?"

Tad's bruised face grew sullen. "I'm not telling *him* anything until I get a lawyer."

Great. Swift mulled it over. "Shouldn't you have one by now? How long is that supposed to take?"

"My mom is trying to hire someone really good."

Swift raked a hand through his hair. "All right." He stood. "I'll be back later."

Tad glanced up. The shadows beneath his eyes looked like bruises. "Are you coming to the funeral, Professor?"

"Not if it will make things harder for you."

"No. It won't. I'd like you there." Tad drew in a shaky breath. "Someone who believes. If it's no trouble." His voice wobbled dangerously.

"I'll be there," Swift promised.

Swift passed Mrs. Corelli on her way to the cells. She

carried a garment bag with a suit for Tad to wear to his father's funeral that afternoon. Swift nodded to her, but she ignored him, staring straight ahead as she followed the deputy, her boots tapping briskly down the chilly corridor.

Swift continued on to Max's office.

Max was on the phone. He nodded in greeting when Swift took the chair in front of his desk. To the person on the other end of line, he said, "What can I say? I don't like it when things are too easy."

Swift stared out the window at the side view of the flagpole forest. The flags were whipping hard in the November breeze, the halyard and pulleys ringing against the metal staff.

Max laughed cheerfully at whatever the caller retorted. "I take that as a compliment... That's right. I take 'em where I can find 'em... Yeah. Later." He stretched forward to replace the handset in the cradle, leaned back in his chair and gave Swift his undivided attention.

"Satisfied?"

"Satisfied how?" Swift asked.

"Satisfied that I kept the police brutality to a minimum?"

Swift had the grace to blush. "Inferred, not implied."

Max snorted. No offense taken.

Swift slid down in his chair, crossed his ankle on his knee. "So what do you think about my theory?"

"You want my answer as the Chief of Police or my answer as the guy who plans to spend the night with you?"

"Are you spending the night with me?"

"If I can get out of here at a decent hour. And if you're not too pissed off to hear that I think your theory is pretty thin."

"I think your theory is pretty thin too. I think a good defense attorney could punch a lot of holes in it. You know

181

why? Because I know firsthand how persuasive a good defense attorney can be. I say this as the guy who was guilty as charged."

Max's smile thinned. "If it helps, I don't think throwing you in jail for some of the stupid things you did would have helped either you or society any."

"I agree. But that's not the point. The point is, you don't have anything in the way of real evidence against Tad other than the fact that he ran, and I think I can explain that to your satisfaction."

"I'm all ears."

Swift took his time explaining about the gay bashing of a kid who was not, in fact, gay.

Max didn't move a muscle until Swift had finished. His chair creaked as he sat upright. "I see. So let me sum it all up for both of us. Depending on my verification of this alleged altercation, you think Tad has an alibi for the time of the murder."

"Er, to be honest, that hadn't occurred to me. I was thinking more about motive."

Max's scarred brow crinkled. He reached for the coffee mug on his desk. "Motive is tricky. See, what might be a good reason for me to kill someone might not be a good enough reason for *you* to kill someone."

Swift stared at his hands loosely clasped around his ankle. "I wouldn't. Deliberately hurt anyone."

"And my impulse is to hurt anyone who hurts you." When Swift's gaze lifted to his, Max said, "See how that works?"

He did, and while it wasn't intended as a compliment, it did warm his heart in a funny way. He managed to joke, "Why, I think that's the most romantic thing anyone's ever said to me."

Max's answering smile was crooked. "That's me. Crazy romantic. Speaking of which, and in answer to your earlier question, yes, just about everyone in the county believes Nerine Corelli is having some kind of relationship with our former mayor. Everyone but our former mayor."

"He could be lying."

"He sure could. But McNeill has a rock-solid alibi for Corelli's homicide."

"What about Nerine's alibi?"

"Same alibi as a matter of fact. They were both campaigning their little hearts out in front of a crowd of potential voters over at Sarah Orne Jewett Elementary School. As a point of interest, they're both on the record as firmly believing the other is behind Corelli's death." Max sipped his coffee. He raised the mug inquiringly, and Swift shook his head.

"What about Mrs. Ord?"

"Mrs. Ord." Max smiled grimly. "That was a good call. Before she was Mrs. Ord, Janine Jensen was Mrs. Paul Jensen."

Swift considered. "Jensen. She's Denny Jensen's mother?"

"Correct. Janine vigorously denies either her son or her son's friends would have access to her keys, but..."

"But?"

"I know guilt when I see it. Janine will be a lot more careful about where she stashes her clients' keys from here on out. It's not proof, but as far as it goes, it makes sense that either Denny or Hodge or even Ariel planted the coke at your place. It always struck me as the kind of thing a vindictive kid might do. Or somebody who wanted—needed—to keep you busy with your own problems and out of theirs."

"It doesn't necessarily connect any of them to the murder."

"No. In fact, it's a leap from planting coke to committing murder."

"Not that big a leap."

"Let's agree to disagree."

Swift grimaced. He thought for a few seconds. "I'm glad you didn't say something like Denny's too young for Nerine."

"Denny's too young for Nerine, but there was as big an age difference between Nerine and Corelli as there was between Nerine and Jensen."

"Anyway," Swift said, "I think you can eliminate Ariel."

"Ariel's the one you threatened to turn in to the cops."

"Ariel wanted to protect Tad. I don't think whoever planted the coke was trying to protect Tad. All that advising him to stay on the run? That was horrible advice."

"It's the kind of advice one kid might give another."

"Not the kind of advice a smart kid would give another. Especially once he heard the story behind Tad's beating, which they all did because Hodge blamed me for Tad's trouble and they all seemed to know what he was talking about."

"You're reaching."

He was, of course. "You're the one who told me Denny was captain of the sailing team in addition to playing football."

Max didn't bat an eye.

His very stillness was a comment in itself. Swift added, just to reinforce his point, "Which means he could have got to and from Orson Island without anyone the wiser."

"*That's* a good point," Max conceded. "It wouldn't be easy to get off that island. I had that dock covered, and we checked the ferry."

"I think Denny, or someone Denny gave a ride to, doubled

back through the woods and headed for the cove behind the bungalow. We didn't think about that because it would be a dead end—unless you had a boat waiting. And you'd only have a boat waiting if you were an experienced sailor."

"Nerine Corelli has an alibi for yesterday afternoon."

"Are you sure?"

Max gave him a chiding look.

"How come she always has an alibi?"

"Hmm." Max scratched his beard. "That's a tough one. She's innocent?"

"I don't buy it."

Max sighed. "I know you don't. But she *does* have an alibi. Also—because I know you're going to bring this up eventually— she's proficient with a rifle. She may know how to use a handgun, but she doesn't own one and, as far as I can discover, no one's ever seen her shoot one."

"So she had an accomplice."

"Bill McNeill also has an alibi for yesterday afternoon."

"That's convenient."

Max didn't bother to reply.

Swift said, "Denny's a little more mature than, say, Hodge or even Tad. I'm not saying he's sophisticated, but he's a personable, attractive young man. I don't know if you noticed he's the same physical type as Mario Corelli."

"Give or take twenty years."

"He seemed genuinely shocked at the idea Nerine Corelli might be having an affair with Bill McNeill."

"A lot of kids are shocked at the idea of people over thirty having sex."

"I think it was more than that."

"I see. Denny takes out Corelli because he and Nerine are having a torrid affair. Do you have some evidence of this affair?"

"No."

"I'm not surprised. We can't find any evidence that Nerine Corelli is having an affair with *anyone*, and believe me, we looked. As far as our investigation indicates, the focus of her life for the past year has been winning this election—which her husband did everything in his power to arrange for her."

"Okay. I give up. Maybe it was the mob."

Max smiled faintly.

"You could still check Denny's alibi. Just for laughs."

"I'm *so* glad I have you to tell me how to do my job."

"Asshole."

Max laughed. He glanced at the clock. "I'm checking everyone's alibi, including Tad's. If you're right and he was busy getting the shit knocked out of him while his father was being murdered, then you've achieved what you hoped to do."

Swift looked up in surprise. "I did, didn't I?"

Max made a sound of amusement. "Yes, Teach. You did. Are you going to Corelli's funeral this afternoon?"

Swift nodded. "I told Tad I would."

The phone on Max's desk rang. From the other room, Hannah shouted, "Max, line three."

As he picked up the phone, Max said to Swift, "Then I'll see you there."

Swift hadn't worn a tie since he'd interviewed for his position at Casco Bay College. He regarded the knot in his navy Hugo Boss tie appraisingly. Serviceable. His father had listed being able to tie a tie as one of those life skills no man should be without. Norris Swift had come from good, solid Yankee stock. New England intellectualism and Old Money.

Swift's memories of his own father's funeral were not clear. This is to say they were dazzlingly, pulsatingly clear—and largely inaccurate, thanks to the fact that he had been stoned throughout. In his mind it had been the most beautiful of spring afternoons. Trembling pink cherry blossoms against a blue butterfly day. The sun chimed gold life. God himself had seemed to read the service in a majestic, booming voice. And what an amazing service it had been, containing as it did all the mysteries of the universe. The many eulogies that followed were equally brilliant and equally moving. It had seemed wonderful to Swift that all his father's friends, both living and dead, had showed up for the occasion.

And so he had told those people, both living and dead—and everyone else who would listen.

At the end of the service he had walked, still babbling, beside his mother to the limo. He had tried to hug her and she had slapped him, once, very hard. It was the only time in his life she ever struck him. Or probably anyone. He didn't begrudge her the slap. Rather the words that had followed.

One thing Marion Gilbert Swift had always possessed was a laser-precise facility with words. Not even his drug-addled wits could protect him from her blame for his father's death, her disbelief and then dismissal of the two years he had managed to stay drug free, her absinthal regret for the accident of his birth, and finally the refusal to let him come to the reception at the house, the refusal to ever have him in her house again.

Swift had long since worked out that she was nearly mad with grief. That half her heart was gone and the other half torn and bleeding.

Old pepper tongue.

Pickles his heart in brine.

The vinegar man is a long time dead.

He died when he tore his valentine.

She had taught him that poem. There was a bit of film somewhere in a long-forgotten documentary of them kneeling together in a patch of sunlight in Norris Swift's study. He was about six, and she was coaxing him into reciting that crazy poem by Ruth Comfort Mitchell. He still remembered her face, young and laughing.

He knew it had not been her intent to destroy him any more than a tsunami targeted an individual victim. He was simply...in her path.

And, let's be honest, he had been a great disappointment for many years.

The next—and last—time he'd seen her had been some months later in court after he had recovered from the overdose that nearly killed him. She'd done her very best to get him institutionalized, but it wasn't an easy thing to do even if you were wealthy, well-known, well-respected, and frighteningly articulate—and even if the "patient" demonstrated what you considered to be self-destructive tendencies.

Drug addiction was not technically insanity, even if it felt like it to everyone concerned.

Swift had not been invited to the wedding when, to the amazement of the literary world, she remarried a couple of years later. He hadn't even known about it until months after. Which was just as well because he wouldn't have begun to know what wedding gift to buy the happy couple.

No. It wasn't funny, but it wasn't tragedy either. They had both survived and life had gone on. Something Swift was quite proud of.

But he didn't like funerals. And he was not looking forward to this one.

Chapter Fifteen

You did not make a choice or follow any direction, but somehow you are descending from space—approaching a great, glowing sphere. It is Edonia, the planet of paradise of which you have heard so much. As your ship slowly descends, you look down on the emerald land and azure waters. Before you is a crystal city sparkling in the sun.

That planet of paradise always did seem like the crackiest of the CYOA books. Choosing not to choose. The philosophy of apathy. Very Zen. What kind of lesson was that? Life didn't work like that. You had to make choices and accept responsibility.

If anyone knew that, Swift did.

It took some people longer than others—and some people never got there at all. He wondered if Nerine Corelli was one of those. He wondered if she regretted any of her choices. She looked composed enough standing there in the front-row pew. He had seen marble effigies look hysterical by comparison.

She had maintained that chilly composure all through the traditional requiem mass, unlike Cora Corelli who Swift had heard sniffing and occasionally sobbing through the hymns.

Tad, in his new suit, stood beside his mother. Ariel, in a demure navy dress that made her look about twelve, stood on his other side. Swift had watched her being snubbed by Cora, but Ariel was made of sterner stuff than some. Swift suspected she and Tad were surreptitiously holding hands out of view of the rest of the congregation. He was glad Max had not handcuffed Tad for the service. For all his toughness, Max could be very kind.

Speaking of Max, he stood in the row of pews behind Tad. At six four, he was hard to miss. Swift's mouth quirked watching the restless twitch of Max's wide shoulders in his brown corduroy suit jacket. Every now and then Max reached up to tug on his tie.

Not much longer now and Max would be out of his misery. And Tad would be back behind bars.

But not for long. Not if his alibi held up. And Swift was sure it would. He knew Max thought it would too.

He glanced around the crowded church—and it *was* crowded. Standing room only. You couldn't move without brushing against someone else.

He tuned back in as the gospel was read. "Jesus said to her, 'I am the resurrection and the life. The one who believes in me will live, even though they die, and whoever lives by believing in me will never die. Do you believe this?'"

They didn't have eulogies in the Catholic Church. Swift thought that was a shame. He'd have been interested in hearing what Mario Corelli's friends and neighbors might have to say about him.

He kept looking until he spotted Bill McNeill. He was in the pew behind Max. Bill didn't look at Nerine Corelli. He didn't look at anyone, as a matter of fact. He kept checking his watch. Maybe he had somewhere to be. What *did* ex-mayors do all day?

One thing for sure, if he was in love with Nerine Corelli, he hid it well.

Anyway, it didn't matter. Not to Swift. Not anymore. Max

was right. He'd achieved what he'd set out to do. He'd helped Tad to the best of his ability.

Beyond that...?

Swift had been keeping an eye out for Denny, but there was no sign of him so far. So maybe he did have that wrong. Not that Swift had a lot of experience at these things, but he felt sure that if Denny was in love with Nerine, he'd have to show up at the funeral. He'd *have* to see her.

Granted, it would be a wee bit awkward going to the funeral of someone you'd murdered. If you were at all inclined toward guilt, this would do it.

Cora gave another of those loud sobs. Tad awkwardly patted her back.

Her grief fascinated Swift. She had seemed to hate Corelli with such a passion, yet there she was weeping away with every evidence of sincerity.

Quite a contrast to Nerine Corelli. Maybe that was part of her incentive.

Detachedly Swift thought about his own death and who would mourn him. Max. Max would certainly mourn him if he died tomorrow. Next month? Maybe not so much. He smiled at himself because he knew that wasn't true. For the first time in a very long time he *was* sure of someone.

And he was sure of himself.

I have come by the highway home,

And lo, it is ended.

Robert Frost, not the Catholic Church, but it seemed appropriate. Swift continued to watch for Denny and instead spotted Hodge standing two rows up from his own position. Hodge's head was bent as he shuffled into the aisle for Communion.

Yes. Everyone seemed to be present except Denny. It might be significant. It might not.

He watched the priest conduct Communion, but his thoughts continued to range far. It didn't matter who had killed Mario Corelli. It had never mattered to him, but he couldn't help wondering. Maybe it was seeing how the death of one person could so affect an entire community.

Cora went up for Communion. Tad and Ariel stayed in the pew. Swift couldn't see Max's face, but he knew from the set of Max's shoulders that he would look grave and alert. It must say something about their relationship that Swift knew Max well enough to know what his expression would be from his stance.

He wondered if one reason his mind was buzzing from thought to thought like an irritated insect was to keep himself from remembering the last funeral he'd been to.

Possibly.

He became aware that the coffin was being carried out and that the mourners were filing into the aisle. He didn't want to get caught behind the crowd. He hated to be hemmed in, hated the crush of people pushing you forward.

Swift edged out into the aisle as quickly as was polite. Turning, he came face to face with Denny Jensen.

Denny looked tired and drawn. He met Swift's eyes and looked briefly startled—as Swift must have done—and then he offered a polite, strained smile before turning away to join the slow train moving from the church.

Swift tried to find Max, but immediately following the end of the service he had gone out the side entrance with Tad and Ariel. There was nothing to do but walk down to the gravesite.

By the time Swift arrived, the priest sprinkled the open

grave with holy water.

"O God, by Your mercy rest is given to the souls of the faithful, be pleased to bless this grave. Appoint Your holy angels to guard it and set free from all the chains of sin and the soul of him whose body is buried here, so that with all Thy saints he may rejoice in Thee forever. Through Christ our Lord. Amen."

Through no effort of his own—in fact he had attempted too late to maneuver himself away—Swift was standing next to Dr. Koltz. Dr. Koltz was as thrilled about that as Swift, and after a tight, uncomfortable nod of greeting, he spent the minutes before the family arrived rocking lightly on his heels and clearing his throat.

Swift listened to the voices and whispers around him. Most people already had Tad tried and sentenced. It began to worry Swift. It was obvious that even if the charges were dismissed against Tad, he would remain guilty in many people's minds.

And people being people, they would show their disgust and disapproval in a million tiny ways. Pinpricks. No mortal wounds, but even a bee sting could kill you if enough bees joined in.

Dropping the charges or insufficient evidence wouldn't be enough for Tad.

It wouldn't be enough for Max either.

Nerine arrived first, local reporters following at a respectful distance. She wore a black cashmere coat and the kind of hat that was more suited to Manhattan than Maine. A rhinestone dragonfly in her coat collar winked in the broken sunlight.

The reporters continued to hang back—though not far—and Nerine took her place at the graveside. Dr. Koltz quit shifting and clearing his throat. Nerine looked across at him and smiled. Dr. Koltz smiled self-consciously back.

Swift happened to be looking straight at Denny Jensen who

was standing as close to Nerine's position as non-family could get, and he saw Denny register the exchange of glances and the smiles.

Denny seemed to lose color. He stared expressionlessly down at the empty grave. His hands twitched and he shoved them in the pocket of his overcoat.

And just like that it was very clear to Swift exactly what had happened.

Well, perhaps not exactly what had happened—but *why* what had happened had happened.

It wasn't Nerine who gave it away. She was cool and lovely and removed as behooved her in her role of society widow. It was Dr. Koltz standing so close to Swift that Swift could practically feel him vibrating. Dr. Koltz was a receiving device and what he was receiving, loud and clear, was Radio Nerine.

And Swift wasn't the only mourner to notice that almost electrical impulse. He could feel people taking unobtrusive stock around him. Dr. Koltz just couldn't seem to help those frequent admiring and sympathetic glances. Testifying more cogently than anything else could that he hadn't a single, solitary clue.

At the foot of the grave Denny grew whiter and whiter.

Cora, Ariel and Tad arrived at last, accompanied by Max.

The priest solemnly intoned the next part of the service.

The news photographers began to snap photos, and with each photo Tad's face grew grimmer and older. It made Swift's heart ache.

Even if Max had left Tad uncuffed, either out of kindness or a sign of faith, it wasn't much protection against that silent censure furrowing, row by row, through the gathering beneath the open green tent.

Tad raised his head and stared defiantly at the crowd.

Swift could feel Dr. Koltz's disapproval as loudly as if he'd spoken it. He didn't speak. However, he gave Nerine another one of those solemn, sympathetic looks.

Poor, dear lady to have to put up with this young thug.

Denny's head jerked up. He glared at Koltz and then he glared at Nerine.

Neither of them took any notice of him.

But Tad did. Tad was staring right at Denny. He was staring at Denny as though he knew...

Swift looked at Max and found that Max was looking right back at him. There was a message in Max's gaze—a possible warning?

There was nowhere to move. Nowhere to go in this press of people. Not without pushing and shoving his way through, and he couldn't do that.

Tad had control of himself again, his face about as revealing as a boulder. He gripped Ariel's hand with a strength that was probably leaving bruises. She grabbed back with equal force.

Swift began to wonder exactly *what* Max had told the kid.

There was a pause for prayers. Heads bowed obediently. The priest began to speak again, but a harsh voice cut across his lilting Irish accent.

"How could you? How the fuck *could* you?"

There was a shocked second or two as the priest's voice fell silent, and then everyone seemed to be speaking at once.

"How dare *you*?" Nerine's outrage was drowned out by Cora's unintelligible response, but Tad wasn't talking to either of them. His comments were addressed to Denny who gaped at him. Denny's mouth moved but no words came out.

Tad roared, "My *dad*? For *her*? For that *bitch*?"

"I don't know what you're talking about," Denny shouted at last. "I told you to keep running."

"Boys! Boys!" Dr. Koltz objected.

Denny turned on him. "Shut the fuck up. Who asked *you*?"

The reporters and photographers were swooping down on them, cameras clicking, voices raised in questions. The priest had recovered his tongue and was making his thoughts on blasphemy known.

Denny began to tug at something in one of the roomy pockets of his coat. Swift watched in fascinated horror. Whatever it was had snagged, and Denny was trying to wrench it free with both hands.

"Dear God," Dr. Koltz exclaimed.

After that, everything seemed to blur. Swift saw Tad lunge for Denny. Ariel threw her arms around him, trying to restrain him. It was left to her because Max had dived through the line of mourners and was wrestling with Denny, whose hand finally extracted a small pistol.

People began to scream and duck down. Denny tried to dislodge Max's grip, swinging the pistol to bear on Dr. Koltz.

Swift acted on instinct, tackling Dr. Koltz and knocking him to the ground. There was a shocking bang and the tang of gun smoke.

Swift waited for the flash of pain, the indication that he'd been shot, but there was nothing but Dr. Koltz heaving and cursing beneath him.

He cautiously raised his head.

Max had Denny's arm yanked up and back at an agonizing angle. The shot had torn through the green canopy, letting in a perfect ray of golden sunlight.

"For future reference," Max said later that evening, "that look does not mean *throw yourself in the line of fire.*"

"How the hell should I know what that look meant?"

There had not been time for conversation after Max disarmed and cuffed Denny. Max had dragged his prisoner off to jail, and Swift had done what he always did these days when reporters started asking him questions. He'd fled.

"Assume from now on that I don't want you jumping in front of anything liable to leave indelible marks." Max hung his coat up and wrapped his arms around Swift. "I hope Koltz appreciated the fact you risked your life for him."

"I admit I did sort of enjoy shoving him." Swift kissed him briskly because he was a little irritated and had had plenty of time to brood on it. "So was that supposed to be your version of ye old wrapping the mystery up in a drawing room? Because I have to say that was a little crude."

"I'm not a drawing room kind of guy. What are you feeding me?"

"Food? Soup. Creamy pumpkin." And at the face Max made, "It's nice. It's made with potatoes and vegetable stock. Anyway, I didn't think I'd see you until a lot later if at all after that stunt today."

"Stunt?" Max followed Swift into the kitchen. "Do I critique your job performance?"

"You know, you could have got your own head blown off. I wouldn't have enjoyed that."

"Me neither."

Swift's glance was unamused. "You repeated to Tad everything I'd said to you, didn't you? You shared my theory."

"After I verified his alibi, yeah, I did. I told him your theory and I watched his reaction, and you know what? He bought it. Hook, line and sinker. I couldn't have asked for better confirmation than to watch him connect the dots. The subconscious is a great tool for getting at the truth."

"You don't think it was maybe a little irresponsible sharing that possibility with Tad right before the funeral? You used Nerine for bait."

"And I'm all broken up over it. Look, I thought it was the fastest way to cut through the bullshit." Max wiped a weary hand across his bristly jaw. Meeting Swift's narrowed gaze, his mouth turned wry. "Okay. And, just between you and me, I did slightly miscalculate. We found the murder weapon in Tad's gym locker, so I underestimated the likelihood of Denny rearming."

"In *Tad's* gym locker?"

"Yeah." Max snorted. "Only problem. It turned up after we'd already searched the locker once."

Swift dumped soup in the saucepan, turned the heat on low and sat down at the table across from Max. "So Denny was having an affair with Nerine Corelli?"

"Not according to Nerine Corelli. According to Nerine she was nice to the kid as she is nice to all her stepson's friends."

"And you believe that?"

Max was silent. "I believe that it'll be all but impossible to prove otherwise. Our mayor is a very canny lady. If she did lead that kid on, there won't be a paper trail or phone records to give her away. Not that we won't look and look hard."

Swift half-closed his eyes, picturing it. "No. She'd plant the suggestion and let Denny come up with the idea all on his own. And then she'd discourage it while letting him think it was actually what she truly wanted."

Max was nodding. "That's the way I see it."

The soup made scorching noises. Swift shoved his chair back and went to stir it. "What does Denny say?"

"That the decision to kill Corelli was his own. That Nerine knew nothing about it."

"Did you ever hear anyone suggest Mario Corelli knocked Nerine around?"

"No. I never did. And I asked plenty."

"I wonder."

"What do you wonder?"

"Maybe she didn't realize how it would end."

Max raised his brows. "Hey, this was *your* theory, remember?"

"I know, but didn't she have basically everything she wanted? Corelli financed her political ambitions. It seems like he would have done almost anything she wanted."

"What she wanted—still wants, I think—is to move up the next rung on the social ladder. That's been her modus operandi all along. From way back when she was Frank Curry's head cashier at Curry's Market."

Swift regarded Max inquiringly.

"Before your time. Frank Curry divorced his wife of twenty years to get engaged to nineteen-year-old Nerine Thompson. But Nerine Thompson jilted him and took a job as hostess at what was then Corelli's Ristorante Familia."

Swift must have still looked blank because Max said, "Who's the biggest of all the big shots in this little college town?"

The light dawned. "Dr. Koltz."

"Dr. Koltz thinks so anyway."

"It hit me during the service that Dr. Koltz and Nerine were having an affair."

Max's smile was sardonic. "Not yet, but today ought to kick start it."

Swift considered this as he poured the piping-hot soup into a black-and-white-striped earthenware bowl.

He carried the bowl to the table and set it in front of Max.

Max watched him, his expression serious. "Nerine is very good at finessing people, but finessing someone like Mario Corelli would be tiring. It's a lot easier to finesse someone like Dr. Koltz."

"I'm still not following. She *was* or she wasn't having an affair with Koltz?"

"Dr. Koltz doesn't have affairs. Not with married women, that's for sure."

"Fairly Machiavellian, isn't it?" Swift was thinking aloud. "She persuades her boy lover to take out her husband so she can then pursue the most eligible bachelor in town."

"Machiavellian. Or *People* magazine. That's why motive is misleading. On the surface, Denny Jensen had nothing to gain by Corelli's death. The truth was, he was willing to do just about anything for Nerine. Including commit murder and frame his best friend for it."

"I guess that explains why Nerine couldn't wait to go to Koltz about my supposedly helping Tad evade justice."

"Yep. You gave her a wonderful opportunity to cry on his shoulder."

"So was Nerine having an affair with Bill McNeill as well?"

"No."

"Then why did everyone think she was?"

"Because she went around hinting to everyone that she was. Bill McNeill told me that, and I believed him because it

201

clearly puzzled the hell out of him."

Swift said thoughtfully, "She wanted people to think she was having an affair with McNeill so they wouldn't notice..."

"Where her real intentions lay."

Swift grimaced. "*Not* with Denny Jensen."

"No. Which even Denny Jensen was bound to notice sooner or later. Which is why he turned up at the funeral with a gun. For him it was love. For Nerine..." Max shook his head and picked up his spoon.

Swift laughed shortly.

"What?"

"Just trying to wrap my mind around the idea of Dr. Koltz inspiring a fatal passion in anyone."

Max choked on his soup and began to cough.

Later when they were upstairs and in bed Swift asked idly, "When you got that anonymous phone call, did it ever go through your mind that maybe I *was* using again?"

Max shook his head.

"Never?"

"The only effort you've made to hide anything from me is that stash of Martha Stewart magazines in the back of your closet. Frankly, if anything was going to scare me off, it would be those magazines."

Swift grinned, but it had been touch and go for a few days there. They both knew that. It made this all the more valuable.

"Who *did* place that anonymous call?"

"Denny isn't saying. I'm guessing Ariel. She wasn't thrilled with you threatening her with the police."

Swift shrugged that off. "Have you ever heard anything

about people wanting me fired?"

Max's brows drew into a dark line. "Seriously?"

"Yes."

"Hell yeah. From the day you were hired."

"Is that true?"

Max nodded.

"I had no idea."

Max shrugged. "Does it matter?"

"Well. It's kind of a weird feeling to know I'm not wanted."

"You're wanted." Max flicked his cheek with the lightest of touches. "*I* want you."

Swift acknowledged it absently, nipping Max's fingertip.

"Why do you think they don't like me? They hired me for God's sake. It's not like there was any mystery about my history."

"I heard you used iambic pentameter once when you should have used a catalexis."

"Huh?"

"Believe me, whatever the reason is, it will make as much sense."

Swift thought this over. Max was probably right, but it was still a weird, unhappy feeling. His mouth curved. "Do you really know what catalexis is?"

"Not a clue. I heard you mention it once. It stuck in my memory because it sounds like a cross between a Cadillac and a Lexus."

Swift chuckled. "You know, you never asked me if I loved you. Did you just take it for granted?"

Max smiled faintly. "No, I wouldn't take that for granted. I do know you well enough to know that if you weren't pretty damned fond of me, I'd have been long gone years ago."

Swift tilted his face to Max's. "I love you. I have for a long time. I'd have mentioned it, but you've always said you weren't into commitment." He added, "Not that love has to mean a commitment."

"Sure it does." Max traced the wing of Swift's eyebrow. "You know what I thought the first time I saw you?"

Swift arched his eyebrow.

"I thought...where did this beautiful, strange guy come from? I thought, no way is he staying in Stone Coast for long."

Swift's mouth quirked. "But that wasn't your only concern."

"No."

Swift acknowledged it without resentment. The fact that they didn't lie to each other was still one of the things he liked best. "But you're not worried anymore?"

"Only in the way everyone worries when you realize someone else's well-being is necessary to your own."

Swift looked into Max's face, the craggy handsomeness that always made his heart skip a beat, the strength admixed by humor and kindness. Funny how he'd only recently come to recognize—and trust—that kindness. He reached up and touched Max's scarred eyebrow as Max had traced his.

"Did you ever catch the guy who did this?"

Max smiled that slow, dangerous grin. "Yep. Sure did."

From beyond the foot of the bed where Max had tossed his jeans, his cell phone rang. Swift groaned.

"You're telling me." Max went to retrieve his phone, clicking it on. "This better be important."

He listened, frowning. The frown grew deeper. His eyes met Swift's. He expelled a long breath.

"Hell." Swift stared moodily back.

"I'll be there as soon as I can." Max clicked off. He shook his head at Swift. "Sorry. I have to go. Judge Vecchio's daughter just got caught breaking into the computer room at Sarah Orne Jewett Elementary."

Swift sighed. "And they say poets keep lousy hours."

"Do they?" Max dressed hurriedly and leaned over the bed. "I shall return. And I'm taking as much of tomorrow off as I can get away with, so plan on sleeping in."

"Sleeping?"

"Whatever."

"I'm holding you to that."

They kissed, warm mouths lingering, and then Max was gone, his footsteps disappearing down the staircase.

Actually what they said was poets were mostly interested in death and commas.

Swift grimaced at the thought and absently watched the painted dolphin swimming through the painted ruins of the mural on the far wall.

The dolphin smiled at him with gentle mischief.

Swift sighed. Safe to say he was going to have to amuse himself for the next couple of hours. He sat up and reached for his own jeans.

Downstairs, he turned the light on in his office and gazed at the stacks of books and papers and file folders. No need to worry about Mrs. Ord's efforts to reorganize his office now. That was too bad. Good help really was hard to find.

Swift sat at his desk and opened the drawer, staring down at the box nestled within.

He lifted the box out. For a time he studied the laminated images of leaves and clouds. It was just a box after all. A pretty box with some scraps of paper in it.

How could something so pretty contain so much fear?

Had he picked it? He didn't remember. Probably not, but it looked like something he'd have liked at one time. Those dancing red and gold leaves against hard, cold blue sky reminded him of illustrations from a favorite childhood book. He didn't remember the book, but he remembered the graceful, muted drawings of nature and the seasons. He remembered his father reading from that book, remembered his father's strong arms around him, his deep, smiling voice reading the words to a beloved child.

He remembered his mother explaining what each leaf was, the slim, smooth hands of a young woman tracing the delicate lines.

He would never hear his father's voice again, and he hadn't seen or spoken to his mother in nearly a decade.

Swift gently stroked the lid of the box. The poems inside might be anything. Might be drug-fueled gibberish. Might be the best thing he'd ever written. Opening this box might be a new beginning. Might as easily be another ending.

He recalled a quote from Butler. *Youth is like spring, an over-praised season more remarkable for biting winds than genial breezes. Autumn is the mellower season, and what we lose in flowers we more than gain in fruits.*

Either way...it was time. He pushed the box aside and reached for the phone, dialing the familiar number.

The phone trilled once, twice...it was late to be calling. How late was it there? Swift was calculating when the receiver lifted. A woman's voice answered from across the miles.

He cleared his throat. "Hi, Mom," said Swift.

About the Author

A distinct voice in GLBT fiction, multi-award winning author Josh Lanyon has written numerous novels, novellas and short stories. He is the author of the critically praised Adrien English mystery series as well as the new Holmes and Moriarity series. Josh is an Eppie Award winner and a three-time Lambda Literary Award finalist.

To learn more about Josh, please visit joshlanyon.com or join his mailing list at groups.yahoo.com/group/JoshLanyon.

SAMHAIN
PUBLISHING

It's all about the story...

Romance

HORROR

www.samhainpublishing.com

CPSIA information can be obtained at www.ICGtesting.com
Printed in the USA
BVOW070525260213

314204BV00001B/27/P